libraries

Parkhead Library
64 Tollcross Road
Glasgow G31 4XA
Phone: 0141 276 1530

This book is due for return on or before the last date shown below. It may be renewed by telephone, personal application, fax or post, quoting this date, author, title and the book number.

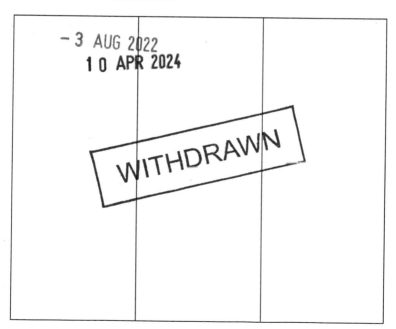

Glasgow Life and its service brands, including Glasgow Libraries, (found at www.glasgowlife.org.uk) are operating names for Culture and Sport Glasgow.

Glasgow
CITY COUNCIL

The Bloody Trail
to Redemption

English aristocrat Born Gallant is riding to Dodge City to meet up with old friends, when he is attacked and left to die. Initially relieved when rescued by a lawman and his posse, Gallant's fortunes take a turn for the worse when his apparent rescuers accuse him of murder. A witness has sworn that he saw him stab the Kansas senator, and it seems certain that Gallant will hang for a murder he did not commit.

Gallant's old friends journalist Stick McCrae and lawyer Melody Lake are able to rescue him from this predicament, but disaster after disaster befall the trio as it becomes increasingly apparent that several people want him dead. A web of political intrigue and vengeance is uncovered, but will Gallant be able to unmask the true murderer before he himself becomes a victim?

By the same author

Encounter at Salvation Creek
The Killing of Jericho Slade

The Bloody Trail to Redemption

Paxton Johns

A Black Horse Western

ROBERT HALE

ISBN 978-0-7198-2038-0

The Crowood Press
The Stable Block
Crowood Lane
Ramsbury
Marlborough
Wiltshire SN8 2HR

www.crowood.com

Robert Hale is an imprint
of The Crowood Press

Typeset by
Derek Doyle & Associates, Shaw Heath
Printed and bound in Great Britain by
CPI Group (UK) Ltd, Croydon, CR0 4YY

ONE

For Born Gallant, the steep ride down through thick woodland some five miles to the south of Dodge City brought back emotional memories, and led to unaccustomed reappraisal and reflection.

It did not for one moment occur to him that it would quickly lead to confrontations with violent men that would test his mettle to its limits.

He had always considered himself to be a hard man with a deceptively mild appearance. A wolf in sheep's clothing, The kind of swashbuckling character who had taken hard knocks playing polo across the green sward of England, then donned the topi and khaki drill of a British cavalry regiment and practised the same horsemanship – replacing the long-handled mallet with a loaded musket – on the barren plains of the Indian sub-continent.

Now it was another untamed frontier, yet the scorching heat filtering down through the canopy of leaves inevitably reminded him of those searing Indian plains and bloody encounters with mutinous sepoys. The similarity did not end with the climate: since relinquishing the title of Lord Gallant of Kent and taking a one-way ticket on a tramp steamer crossing the Atlantic, he had been involved in several violent skirmishes in this wild land to the West of the Mississippi River.

He was a crack shot with rifle and pistol, an excellent swordsman who was also a dangerous opponent in a knife fight. When it suited him, he adopted an aristocratic English accent to confuse lawmen and outlaws by playing the upper-class twit. The time gained had more than once saved his life in the Wild West. Even so, he might have come a cropper on several occasions had it not been for the help of Kansas newspaperman Stick McCrae and the delightful young Melody Lake. But he had prevailed, had emerged from the gunsmoke of battle unscathed and without staining the grass of the American West with his blue blood. Well, the occasional drip here and there, he thought, with a buccaneering grin. Nothing fatal, or he wouldn't be atop a fine horse, in these damn sweltering woods, doing some serious thinking – what?

The big gelding he had bought from a livery barn in Wichita was picking its own way down the slope through tangled undergrowth and a treacherous carpet of dead leaves. Gallant's lean frame was tipped back in the saddle. The reins were held loosely in his gloved hands, his sharp blue eyes ranging from side to side. His was a ride with a dual purpose. The first part was to spend time in Dodge with Stick and Melody, and the second had followed naturally; leaving the trail to cut through the woods was a minor inconvenience, but he had been here before. Six months ago? He'd escaped by the skin of his teeth from a Dodge City posse after the killing of Jericho Slade, led a poor kid he'd rescued from a necktie party to what Gallant had considered to be safety – and it had all gone wrong.

There. His eyes, narrowed now, had lost all warmth.

A few yards down the hill he had spotted the tree where the kid, Billie Flint, had taken a rifle bullet in the back. The youngster's body had lost all strength. He had sagged against that tree, then gone down, his eyes glazed in death. On foot, knowing there was nothing he could do for the kid, Gallant had clawed his way uphill. He'd pulled away from the lawmen, gaining precious yards. Over the ridge he had flung himself into a dry gully and buried himself under dead leaves.

The talk he heard, as the men searched to the very edge of his hiding-place, told him that if he was found, he would die. So he had waited until he heard the men move away, then worked his way back down a stony creek-bed on the outskirts of the woods. There, with the image of the dying Billie Flint driving him on, he had with considerable violence taken care of the man left on guard.

Somewhere, far down the slope, a horse whinnied.

Memories fluttered away like frightened birds. Gallant, now moving away from the tree where Flint had died, felt a twinge of unease. At once he knew it was illogical. Sight of the tree, the sickening memory of blood-soaked clothes, of a young man's eyes filming as he breathed his last – all this had put his nerves on edge. The woods were hot, airless, oppressive. Gave a person the jitters. Put the wind up a man, but for no reason.

And yet ...

The creek was away to his left.

He turned his horse and rode out of the woods. Away from the shelter of the trees he was hit by the full force of the midday sun. The gelding's hoofs rattled on the loose stones. Dust rose from a water course that in winter would be a raging torrent but was now like a gully in the Sahara desert. It sloped down, snaking along the edge of the trees.

Memory again came flooding back to chill Gallant's soul.

The last time he had come down this slope he had been on foot. That had made his descent much quieter. The lawman leading the posse had left a man with the horses. He was waiting at the bottom of the slope, away from the trees, his back turned as he paced and smoked a cigarette: there for the taking. Gallant had pounced like a cougar, suffered a bloody nose for his trouble but he'd ground the man's face into the soft earth until he went limp, unconscious – or dead.

On this occasion his luck seemed to have run out.

Born Gallant cursed softly.

There were two of them. Tough characters on horseback, their rifles flashing in the sun. Hard eyes

8

were fixed on Gallant. He drew rein, pinned by the aim of the rifles' muzzles. One of the men, tall, unshaven, flashed a glance at his companion. He, stockier, with muscles that strained his shirt and vest, was nodding slowly. They had waited, followed with sharp ears the noise of a horseman's descent through the woods and down the dry creek. For all they knew it could have been anyone: a drifter, a saddle tramp, a hunter heading for home.

But the silent exchange of glances told Gallant that he had been identified. They did know who he was. More than that, they had been expecting him; even in that moment when he thought it quite possible that his life hung by a slender thread, he wondered how that could be.

The heat beat down. No words were spoken. The silence was tense. It was as if the two men were again waiting.

Won't last, Gallant thought, mind racing. But what could he do. He'd heard the horse whinny, damn it, a warning he should have heeded. But he had not been expecting trouble. And now...?

Ignoring the rifles he twisted in the saddle. He was still on the creek's rocky bed. There were two ways he could go. Back, and risk taking a couple of bullets between the shoulder blades. Or forward, charging at the two men like a crazed steer in the hope that the shock of the move would see them freeze for long enough to allow him through to the open grassland, where in any race he would fancy his chances.

Then stones rattled higher up the creek. The net

tightened, then closed as a third man came into view. He was raw-boned, rangy, riding a proud chestnut thoroughbred gelding. Beneath a flat-crowned black hat, dark-brown hair liberally streaked with grey tumbled to his shoulders. His face appeared to have been carved from rock by a chisel that had cut with bold strokes and left the edges of cheekbones and jaw unfinished. His eyes were of that kind of blue that appears white in certain lights and can be confused with blindness. In certain situations that would be an advantage, Gallant thought, when this man clearly needed none: the horse he rode told of money in the bank, and even the stupidest of men with little experience of life would know that they were looking at a killer. *That's the rub*, Gallant thought ruefully. The only way out of this might have been to ride straight across the dry creek. But the far bank was fully eight feet high with a deep and crumbling undercut; now, even without that insurmountable obstacle, this man's sudden appearance meant that it was far too late for flight.

'A pleasure to meet you gents on this fine summer's day,' Gallant said jauntily, 'but afraid I can't hang about chewing the fat. Places to go, things to do, don't you know, got a journalist pal—'

'Shut up.'

The first words. They came from the new arrival, and cracked like a whip. Even as the thought came to Gallant, he saw that this lean, hungry-looking man bearing the stink of death was carrying just that: his hands were folded easy on the saddle horn, but in those gloved fists there was a wicked-looking rawhide whip. The handle was a foot of plaited leather, probably with a core of hardwood. The short lash tapered from the handle, hung straight down, the tip brushing the man's left boot. It was weighted by what appeared to be a big knot tied to prevent the leather from fraying.

Ghastly implement of torture, Gallant thought, thinking bleakly of the cat o' nine tails that on the Indian plains had tickled more than one soldier's shoulders. This whip was about to dish out some of the same, no doubt. But why? Well, his was not to reason why, his was but to do or die, and so on and so forth. It seemed that a straight fight was out of the question. He had his six-gun, a rifle in its saddle boot, but going for either of them would be suicide. Deciding that the best he could do would be to make 'em think he was short of a few brain cells – put 'em off guard – he dug deep but could come up with nothing better than a foolish grin.

The man on the thoroughbred shook his head, met the grin with a derisive half-smile. He transferred the whip in his left hand. With his right he drew his six-gun, and thumbed back the hammer.

'I'll keep him covered,' he said to the two gunmen, 'but take care. This feller's cunning and dangerous, as my poor brother would confirm if he had breath in his body and could talk from the inside of a coffin.' He let the words hang in the heat, watching Gallant as if waiting for a response. Then, realizing nothing was forthcoming, he said, 'All right, put away your rifles

11

and get him strung up.'

Not a chance, old boy, Gallant thought, teeth gritted. *Nobody's stringing me up, so it's now or never, up and at 'em.*

With a jerk of both heels he raked the gelding with his spurs.

The horse squealed in protest, then shot forward. Gallant drove his mount straight at the two gunmen. But there his plan fell apart. The move had been expected, the distance to be covered was too great. The men had time to ease their horses to one side. They separated, leaving an inviting gap. Even as Gallant seized the moment and spurred between them he knew he had been outfoxed. The rifle held by the leaner of the two men was a silvery blur as he swung it at Gallant's head and knocked him out of the saddle.

TWO

Consciousness returned to Gallant with a blaze of agony that was pure-white heat. The sun was high overhead, a little way behind him, but they had taken away his hat and his thick blond hair was a hot skull-cap torturing his scalp. Under that cap his head ached fiercely from the blow that had knocked him sense-less. He'd been stripped to the waist, shirt and plain hide vest ripped from his body. His torso and face were burning. The intense glare was turning his closed eyelids bright pink.

Gasping for air, struggling to breathe, he realized he was hanging by his arms. Rawhide thongs were biting into his wrists. He could feel the warm trickle of blood. The extreme position and his own dead weight were restricting the movement of his ribs, his diaphragm. Relief could come only by taking the weight off his arms. That was impossible. Try as he might, he could not touch the ground with his toes. He gave that up, tensed his arm and shoulder muscles and pulled his body higher. For a few moments there was blessed relief. Then the strain became too great. Mentally and physically he sagged. Once again, drawing breath became nigh on impossible.

Gallant opened his eyes.

He was facing the undulating grassland that he knew stretched away to the rails of the Atchison, Topeka and Santa Fe railroad, and the town of Dodge City. His eyelids fluttered. In front of him, two silent watchful men on horseback. Two? Hadn't there been three? He forced his hanging body into a twisting mid-air dance that brought a stifled groan from between clenched teeth. He could see left, then right. No third man. Locking his shoulders to stop the twisting, the pain clearing his head and bringing back memory, he squinted at the men in front of him.

One was the unshaven, leaner of the two gunmen. He was looking away, appearing uninterested as he smoked a cigarette. The other was the big man on the thoroughbred gelding. But his demeanour, too, had changed. The confidence was there in abundance, but no longer was he snapping curt instructions while holding Gallant at the point of a gun. The opulent-looking, bone-handled pistol was back in its holster. His hands were folded on the saddle horn.

Not only watchful, but waiting, Gallant thought.

For what?

And where the hell was his whip?

The answer, like the return of consciousness, came in a blaze of agony as the lash cracked across Gallant's naked back and the big knot curled around his ribs and bit into his chest.

*

He had no awareness of the passing of time. At some point in the vicious flogging his body closed down, sensitive nerve ends deadened in a pure survival instinct. From the comfortable refuge in his brain to which his consciousness had fled, Gallant was vaguely aware that the man standing behind him to wield the whip was placing each cruel stroke with care. Choosing unmarked skin. Raising ugly red weals, no doubt, but not drawing blood. The aim was to inflict the maximum pain without leaving permanent scars, Gallant thought. But why the torture? And why did the big man on the thoroughbred want him to live?

The beating came to an end. For what seemed like an eternity there had been a stroke of the whip, a space, then another stroke. Then Gallant, eyes closed, lids gummed by salt sweat, became aware that after the last stroke there was just the space. Then voices came to him as mumblings, the words indistinguishable. His nostrils flared to the tang of cigarette smoke. Someone laughed. There was the cooling sound of water splashing from a flask, awakening Gallant to his terrible thirst, and he moaned and licked dry lips with a tongue already swelling.

Bridles jingled. There was what sounded like a gruff command. Hoofs beat on the hard ground, faded. As the three men rode away, Gallant was enveloped in silence. It was broken by the buzz of insects, the flutter of birds' wings, their excited twittering as they returned to perch in the branches of trees covering the hillside at his back.

But it was the other birds that worried Gallant, those big birds that soared and circled at a great height, had sharp eyes and hooked beaks and were uncannily sensitive to the smell of impending death.

As he slowly emerged from the mental hibernation that had enabled him to come through a beating that might have put a fatal strain on weaker hearts, Gallant was again assailed by pain. From his bleeding wrists to his impossibly stretched and strained shoulders, from his throbbing head to a back that felt as if it had been dragged repeatedly across rusty barbed wire, he was in torment.

Treatment was needed for all the wounds deliberately, callously inflicted, but there was none available. Escape was impossible. His wrists were bound with rawhide: had they soaked the leather first, knowing it would dry and tighten? His feet were swinging well clear of ground; his body was too damn heavy for tortured muscles to lift. He'd hang there, then; suffer, until help arrived or Hell froze over. That icy thought cheerfully reminded him that while the flogging had not brought him close to death, the searing sun might finish the job. Or perhaps not. Time had moved on. The sun had drifted south, and Gallant was now hanging in the shadows cast by the trees at his back.

Time then, to wait and endure. And wonder. Wonder for however many hours lay ahead just how and why three armed and dangerous men could have been lying in wait for him at the end of a ride that was never a secret, but had not been discussed with friend or foe.

Nevertheless his intention to ride had become known to men of ill will.

Where had he inadvertently revealed his plan?

As far as the dazed and suffering Gallant could work out it would be pointless sending his thoughts further down his back trail than to Wichita. Once that decision had been made his mind found some focus and the answer leaped out at him with the speed of a striking rattler.

Passing through that stinking hell-hole of a cattle town he had eaten in a familiar smoke-filled café close to Rowdy Joe's dance hall, had skimmed through the latest edition of the *Wichita City Eagle*, had then wiped his hands on the newspaper and moved on to the Buckhorn saloon. There, drink in hand and one foot on the brass rail, he had got into conversation with a rough-looking character who'd drunk enough to make standing difficult. However, though one hand kept a tight grip on the oak bar, beneath the sweat-stained black Stetson the man's eyes were clear and intelligent. He'd studied Gallant without turning his head, watching his reflection in the ornate, fly-blown mirror. Then he'd nodded thoughtfully.

'Englishman,' he said. 'Name of Gallant. Saw you in Dodge, read about you in the *Dodge Times*.'

'Not saying you're right or wrong,' Gallant said, 'but aren't you somewhat garrulous for a Westerner? Conversation before introduction, that sort of thing.

Likely to put you in a spot of bother if the listener takes offence, wouldn't you say?'

'And you say I'm garrulous?' The man turned to face him. 'Yeah, I know what that word means. Used to work alongside Stick McCrae on the *Kansas City Star*. Come to think of it, your name cropped up there. Both times I heard it, you were in trouble with the law.'

'Actually, old chap,' Gallant said, 'the law was having some trouble with me.'

'A big 'breed died at Salvation Creek; a while after that a lawman name of Dolan got his comeuppance in Dodge. I hear he lost a leg, which annoyed him somewhat. You're poison, feller, so why stick around?'

'Is that a threat?'

'Hell, no. I told you, I use a pen, not a gun.'

'Words are your business?'

'Right. I tell stories.'

'Juggle fact and fiction till indistinguishable? Something tells me I should take anything you say with a pinch of salt.'

'Which is a polite way of calling me a liar.'

The man tossed back another shot of whiskey, pursed his lips, beckoned for a refill.

'Nobody stays long in Wichita,' he went on after some thought. 'Give or take a mile here and there, this town's 'bout as far south of Ellsworth as it is to the east of Dodge City. Can't recall the name Gallant connected to violent death in Ellsworth, so either you're losing your touch, or there's no excitement. My money says you're heading for Dodge.'

'The newspaperman with no name rolls the dice. Is he a winner?'

'It's Chet Eagan.'

'Well, Eagan, you've won but there's no story in it for you. I'll be in Dodge looking up your old colleague, McCrae. On the way – seeing as I'm in the area – I'll cut through woods to the south of the town where a young man died.'

'Billie Flint. For a time word was you killed him.'

'Nothing like a good rumour,' Gallant said, 'to send vindictive fools chasing their own tails.'

And with that, he'd downed his drink and walked away from Eagan.

He drifted in and out of consciousness. Most times when he came back it was to suffer unbearable pain in his back, shoulders and wrists, and in those moments he craved the return of soothing blackness. But there was a time when his senses returned and he realized he was shivering, that the sun was well down and that it was quite likely that his temperature was soaring. That disturbed him and also set him chuckling crazily through clenched teeth: he had survived a cruel flogging while suspended by his wrists from a high tree – and now he was worried about a mild fever. Then, as the bubbling laughter subsided to be replaced by barely stifled groans, he heard the rattle of hoofs, heralding the approach of several riders. Time to regain control. He drew several shuddering breaths. Willed the red throbbing pain to the back of his mind. Opened his eyes.

19

The first thing that caught his eye, glittering in the light of the setting sun, was the tin badge on the lead man's vest.

'Praise the Lord for the cavalry,' he managed through swollen lips. 'Come galloping over the ridge to rescue me, and not before time. Be a decent chap and cut me down, would you? Suffering mild discomfort, don't you know, so release and a splash of water would be most beneficial.'

'Do as he asks,' the lawman said.

He watched dispassionately as two of his men swung down.

They approached Gallant. A third man rode over, reached up with a knife and slashed through the rawhide that was strained taut between Gallant's wrists and the overhead bough. Gallant dropped like a stone. He'd been suspended no more than a foot from the ground. His legs supported the sudden weight of his body – just. He wobbled, staggered, felt his knees begin to give and was steadied by the men at his side. Then, muttering thanks, he lowered his arms. A big mistake. The agony in his shoulders was like a red-hot iron searing the end of every tortured nerve, every strained and torn tendon. Somewhere in his head there was a fierce crackling. Then, once again, he blacked out.

He was flat on his back when consciousness returned.

The man down on one knee, bending over him, was Stick McCrae.

'Might have known you'd show up,' Gallant

croaked, forcing a grin. 'Must admit I didn't notice Melody in that bunch of glum-faced ruffians who cut me down.'

'It's a posse,' McCrae said. 'She's not here, and I didn't just show up. I'm here under editor's orders. I'm the scribe assigned to write details when a hunted killer is arrested in woods south of Dodge. The story'll be in tomorrow's edition of the *Dodge City Times.*'

'You're confident they'll catch him?'

'You could say that.'

'Pull me up, Stick, but go easy on the shoulders.'

The manoeuvre was achieved with relative ease. From a sitting position in the grass Gallant saw that the posse's half-dozen riders were standing by their horses, talking and smoking. The tall lawman was a little apart. He was watching McCrae.

'One swift look at my back will tell you why I was strung up shirtless,' Gallant said. 'But the wicked beating has raised questions I cannot answer, the main ones being why me, and what kind of twisted game were those fellers playing? In particular, a mean-looking individual with hair touching his bony shoulders and eyes like winter ice.' He thought he detected a flicker of interest, of recognition of the description, in McCrae's eyes, then deliberate blankness.

'Well,' Gallant went on, 'those questions must wait. What the beating didn't do was damage the lion's heart that beats within my tormented frame, but it has left my impressive strength impaired. I can't ride with you, Stick. When they find the killer and you pen your prose, I'll be on the way to Dodge City and the nearest doc.'

'The killer's found.'

'Already? So why waste time with me? Throw me on a horse, then go with the posse when they make the arrest.'

'Sometimes,' Stick McCrae said wearily, 'your valiant attempts at light-hearted banter blind you to the obvious.'

'Can't argue with that,' Gallant said, 'but it's pretty clear that marshal over there is getting itchy. Allowed you to talk to me, but all he can see you doing is wasting time.'

'His name's Cole Banning. Banning was a deputy in Kansas City. They transferred him to Dodge to replace Liam Dolan.' He looked hard at Gallant. 'D'you remember the senator for Kansas?'

'Morton J. Slade? We found his son's killer. Not something easily forgotten.'

'One of those touchy-feely politicians, liked meeting folks, being seen as one of 'em. A couple of days ago he was crossing Kansas by stagecoach, getting close to the people, shaking hands, kissing babies. Two marshals were riding shotgun. On a barren stretch of scrubland in the middle of no-damn-where the driver pulled the coach to a halt for a smoke break. Five minutes later the two marshals were dead, shot in cold blood from a distance by someone possessing uncanny skill with a rifle. Slade was enjoying a cigar, both the coach's doors open to let in some more of what was mostly hot air—'

'That a joke?'

'Unintentional.' McCrae smiled bleakly. 'When Slade realized what was going on and courageously stepped down from the coach, a rider on a rangy horse was closing in fast. According to the stage's driver – a feller still struggling to come down off his seat – Slade appeared to recognize him, thought help had arrived. That was his undoing. The man piled down off his horse, moved in close and made as if to shake hands. Then he drew what the driver reckoned was a Bowie knife from a sheath in the small of his back. Killed the senator with a single thrust to the heart.'

'First the son dead, now the husband.' Gallant pulled a face. 'The grief Slade's poor wife must be experiencing is unimaginable: could be three lives finished, not two. But why are you telling me now?'

'Because most of the Dodge City folk, and all of those wearing badges,' McCrae said, 'are convinced the senator's killer was a madcap English aristocrat by the name of Born Gallant.'

THREE

When, some months earlier, Born Gallant had snatched Billie Flint from the necktie party and a looming gallows, it had been at some remove from the cell where the kid had been held prisoner. In the early morning on the main street there had been sunlight to brighten spirits, cleanse the soul and inspire optimism. To say that Gallant had not thought about those other grim conditions in the cell would be to stretch a point: he looked at the kid being marched from jail to gallows, saw the youngster's drawn countenance and the cornhusks clinging to his wrinkled clothes and knew that the accommodation had been primitive, the food maggoty and fit only for rats. But his thoughts had not lingered. At the time he'd been too intent on confusing those who were of the necktie party with eccentric play-acting. It included convincing them that he and the kid were related and deserved a last, emotional reunion.

Now, just how primitive those Dodge City cell conditions were had been brought home to him with a down-to-earth jolt. After the long hot ride from the woods he was dragged from his horse and through the jail office to be thrown without ceremony on to a hard dirt floor. From there, curled into a ball to avoid expected brutal kicks that weren't delivered, gritting his teeth against intolerable pain, he listened to the clang and clatter of a barred door being slammed and locked. It was followed by some harsh words he couldn't make out, and the scrape and thud of departing boots.

He was still naked from the waist up, soaking from the waist down. At some point on the ride he'd been dragged from his horse and thrown into the cold waters of a tumbling creek: the theory being, he supposed, that such crude washing of the red weals raised by the big man's whip helped prevent the onset of infection that might lead to his death. That was to be avoided at all costs, Gallant had thought wryly: they wanted him alive, so that they could string him up – and next time, if what Stick McCrae had told him was truly the way folk were thinking, it would not be by the wrists.

He lay on the hard floor with his thoughts as tangled as mesquite brush, breathing shallowly of fetid air and losing all track of time as he slipped in and out of consciousness. Eventually, as the hot Kansas day dragged on, he roused himself enough to crawl on hands and knees to the crude bunk and claw his way up on to the relative comfort of a thin mattress. Then came another period of sleep that was as near as dammit to a full coma, leading to the eventual realization as senses returned that he was shivering like a man with ague. The sun, he surmised, had long gone down. The evening was cooling and, as if to mock his plight, a chill breeze was whispering through the high barred window to bring painful goose bumps to his naked back.

Dying, Gallant thought. Worst of all, he was going out like a cowed dog. Following that defeatist thought, in a fiery flash there came a rapid flickering mental replay of all the campaigns he'd survived on several continents, each triumph achieved through his own indomitable spirit: the quality he'd jocularly referred to when in dire straits as, *Never say die, old sport, that's the ticket, what?* That thought, madcap though it might sound, brought an immediate response. Flat out on a stained cornhusk mattress, Born Gallant let go a shattering bellow of rage. Such was the volume of his fury, he later swore to Stick McCrae, that, like an array of tuning forks, the very cell bars hummed in a vibrant musical response.

Then he dragged up the thin blanket so that it covered him from ankles to shoulders, and drifted away into deep, untroubled sleep.

'Wounds or no wounds, they'll move you out, and fast,' McCrae said. 'You murdered Senator Morton J. Slade, a respected political figure who's overcome tragedy. There'll be a show trial in the state capital.'

'And a public execution, otherwise why take me all that way?' Gallant frowned. 'Slade dead, both men guarding the senator's coach drilled by a skilled man with a rifle, so the stagecoach driver was the only man left standing. He must be the man who identified me.'

'Reckons he recalls you from when you were last in Dodge. Hair the colour of bleached straw, cool blue eyes, insolent swagger. He swore on the Bible.'

'It's a put-up job, and it stinks to high heaven. Hell, you know that, Stick; you wrote the original story. Six months ago a senator's young son was shot dead on a busy street. I risked my life to find the kid's killer. Turned out be Liam Dolan, the town's marshal. You and Melody helped me dump him on the senator's doorstep.'

'After I shattered his knee with a bullet. Don't know if you're aware, but he lost that leg soon after, died from gangrene.'

'Unlamented. You saved my life, but capturing him put a feather in *my* cap. Why would I return, and kill the senator?'

'You can be sure they'll come up with a damn good reason.'

'They?'

McCrae shrugged. Seated on the edge of the bunk, elbows on his knees and lean hands dangling, the newspaperman looked deeply worried. Gallant knew him well. He was a persistent newshound, and must have come up with a plausible story for Cole Banning that gained him admittance into the cell. Interview with doomed man, that sort of rot. That he had made his way in was a credit to his ingenuity, and Gallant was grateful, and impressed.

'Even if we had the names,' McCrae said, 'we'd be

27

struggling. I told you Dolan died of his wounds, so the easy answer is Liam Dolan's kin.'

'The fellow with the whip said something about his brother talking from the inside of a coffin.'

'But if Dolan's kin were looking for revenge, they'd likely have put a bullet in your back one dark night. It'd be over in the crack of an unseen rifle, and you'd have died easy. But this way. . . ?'

'Morton J. Slade died from a knife thrust to the heart.' Gallant twisted on the cot, wincing as the raw wounds criss-crossing his back began to tear. 'Couple of days later I get the punishment usually meted out to an English seaman sailing before the mast.'

'I don't like jumping to conclusions,' Stick McCrae said, 'but it's possible someone had it in for both you and the senator. So we need to find if there's anything linking you, Slade and the killer.'

'A slight handicap, Stick: I'm locked in a cell.'

'But about to be moved. If one man can coolly gun down two guards and murder a senator, another not too far away from your good self can surely work out a way of rescuing the man likely to hang for his crime.'

Suddenly, Gallant was grinning. 'Knew deep down that when I snatched Billie Flint there'd be repercussions. 'Pon my soul, writing that story corrupted you, Stick, hardened your tender heart and opened your innocent eyes to all kinds of lawless activities.'

'To use one of your words, that's poppycock. A while back, in Kansas City, you walked into your room and found me sitting on the bed threatening you with a '73 Winchester. I've already pointed out it was me downed Liam Dolan—'

'Ah, but then you were a law-abiding citizen righting a terrible wrong.'

'—and innocence leaves most journalists when they learn that words, true or false, can be dangerous weapons.'

'Point taken. You showed your mettle in Salvation Creek. What bothers me now is the thought of the lovely Melody Lake riding alongside you when you take on an armed escort.'

'Melody,' McCrae said, 'has returned to Kansas City to pursue her career as a lawyer.'

'Praise the Lord,' Gallant said fervently. 'If you fail miserably in your valiant attempt to rescue that innocent man, at least he'll have one lawyer free and on his side when it comes to a trial.'

FOUR

Light-hearted conversation with a genial companion, even in the worst of circumstances, can flood the soul with the sun's warmth and lift a weary man's flagging spirits. When that chat, moreover, raises the possibility of a daring escape from – as Gallant put it – a sticky situation, then so much the better.

Unfortunately, the way it turned out it was so much the worse.

After a night spent lying with what felt like sharp rocks digging into his most sensitive parts, in the discomfort of a cold cell that stank of everything from cat pee to lingering memories of male flatulence, Gallant hadn't been fool enough to expect breakfast. What he had looked forward to was a fast move from Dodge City's dehumanizing jail accommodation in something like a Concord stagecoach that, on the trip to Kansas City, would at least afford shelter from the midsummer sun.

What he got was an ancient buckboard. Not the finest of its kind. Gallant's immediate assessment was that the wagon had spent the whole of the War

Between the States transporting too many soldiers over very long distances, then for years had been left out in all weathers.

From his office desk, where a cup of hot coffee steamed at his elbow, Marshal Cole Banning watched impassively as two burly deputies dragged Gallant bodily from the cell. They threw him on to the waiting buckboard's flat top, still without a shirt, but with what felt like a stiff, unwashed horse blanket thrown over his shoulders. Then both deputies leapt aboard, one touched the horse with a flick of the whip and the wagon rocked and jolted across the railway tracks that bisected Front Street.

Their destination was a workshop behind a row of humble business premises. From a low-roofed interior where sparks flew in dazzling showers, Gallant could hear the sound of hammer ringing on anvil. The now stationary buckboard rocked to a heavy weight. Gallant was enveloped in a shadow the equivalent of a full solar eclipse and felt the comparatively comfortable kiss of cool iron. A face was grinning at him from inches away. Black eyes glittered above a tangle of beard in which ravens might have nested unseen.

The two lawmen held him. Blunt fingers ripped off Gallant's boots and socks, gripped his bare legs. Using two sledgehammers, thick bands of metal and a lot of noise, the blacksmith fitted an iron fetter around each of Gallant's ankles. They were connected by a short chain.

'Skilful chappie,' Gallant said with genuine admiration. 'Rest assured I'll recommend you to all my

31

equine chums in need of the odd shoe.'

The blacksmith's eyes narrowed in incomprehension, or perhaps suspecting an insult. He turned and spat. One of the deputies laughed.

'You finished there?'

'*He's* finished,' the blacksmith said. 'Bending those things around his legs is one thing. Gettin' them off again is another matter entirely. If he ain't hanged, he'll be wearin' 'em the rest of his life.'

And yet—

Maybe he had a bit of grit in his eye. Or a twitch, a tic he couldn't control. But as the big man glanced back at his victim before turning away to jump down from the buckboard, Gallant was quite sure he saw an eyelid flicker in what could only have been a conspiratorial wink.

Though now wearing boots cut down by the blacksmith's knife to accommodate ironwork that would turn his walking gait into the mincing strut of one of Dodge's painted saloon girls; with the skin of his back criss-crossed by livid healing scars, and the only cover protecting him from the rising sun a filthy blanket probably scorned by the horse, Born Gallant's face was the picture of contentment.

His teeth were clicking, not from cold, but from the jolting of the buckboard as it was driven at considerable speed down a track resembling a field furrowed by an inexperienced nester with a lame horse and blunted plough. The boards of the buckboard's flat bed were splintered and warped; changing his position wasn't worth the effort, and he knew for certain that when he reached Kansas City his backside would be black and blue.

Yet still, on his face, there was a half-smile.

Gallant had complete faith in Stick McCrae. He knew that the buckboard was never going to make it to Kansas City. They had left Dodge City travelling in a roughly north-easterly direction. From Dodge to Kansas City was a good 300 miles, and in covering that distance they would have needed to make overnight stops at towns such as Ellsworth and Abilene. As it was, they made forty miles – with one rest stop – before the lawman at the reins was forced to wrench the buckboard to an unexpected and abrupt halt that kicked up a billowing cloud of dust.

They were first alerted by the rattle of hoofs on the hard ground, the source hidden by straggly trees. Then, ahead of them, a glossy chestnut mare had come galloping around a bend in the trail. It was being ridden by a young woman. When they did see her they were stunned by the sheer ferocity of her riding. So much in a hurry was she that she abandoned the trail and cut across the bend, bringing her wild-eyed mount crashing through undergrowth and low-hanging branches. She finished up back on the rutted trail with her mount rearing close to the now stationary buckboard and her own eyes wide with excitement.

'Go back,' she cried, with difficulty restraining the excited mare. 'They're waiting, not half a mile away. They're going to set Gallant free, take him from you—'

'Ma'am, slow down for just a minute,' said the deputy who was riding shotgun. 'Who's waiting? How many of 'em? And, ma'am, don't I know you from somewhere?'

'I'm Melody Lake,' the woman said, 'and of course you know me, I work for the *Dodge City Times* and that means you should trust me.' *You've played this game before, you wonderful, lying little firebrand,* Born Gallant thought with a frisson of pure joy.

'Ma'am, even if I trust you, going all that way back just on your say-so is—'

'Oh, you will be going back,' another voice cut in, 'but when you do you'll be taking an empty buckboard.'

Both lawmen spun round on the high seat. Gallant, lying painfully behind them on the rough boards, twisted more slowly. Like the lawmen, he'd recognized the sound of a shotgun being cocked. He'd also recognized the voice, and was filled with admiration for McCrae and Lake.

A pretty woman had ridden a circular route to put her ahead of the stagecoach and create a diversion, appearing flushed and flustered as she delivered a stark warning.

A man riding at a cautious distance had followed the buckboard all the way from Dodge. Timing his move to coincide with the woman's act, he had closed in like a ghost from the rear carrying a weapon against which six-guns were of no more use than a child's slingshot. Confident of their success, he had called first at the Dodge livery barn, collected Gallant's gelding and brought it along for the prisoner he was determined to set free.

'McCrae?' There was disbelief in the lawman's voice. 'You and Lake, hell, you're both respectable citizens – but this madness'll get you ten years in the state pen.'

'Quit wasting your breath and unbuckle your gunbelt, Madison. Deacon, you do the same, then raise your hands and keep 'em reaching.'

Tight-faced, both men hesitated for long moments in which the tension mounted – then they complied. Gunbelts were unbuckled. They thudded to the boards at their feet. In a rush of movement Melody Lake brought the mare in close. Leaning down from the saddle she scooped up the weapons then moved away.

'Stick, bringing my horse along showed you put a lot of thought into this,' Gallant said. 'Trouble is, when we ride away from here I'll be lying over the beast belly-down.' He lifted both legs stiffly and waggled them to set the short chain clinking and reveal his plight.

'Sidesaddle,' Melody Lake said, smiling sweetly at Gallant as she drew back her arm and sent the lawmen's gunbelts crashing deep into the scrub. 'Isn't that the way your blue-blooded lady friends canter across English meadows, chasing foxes?'

'I've got a better idea,' McCrae said. He slid the shotgun into its boot, then brought his horse alongside the buckboard. He loose-tied the spare mount to the sideboards, then stepped from saddle to wagon.

'Melody, keep those fellers covered. Born, stretch out your legs, flat against the boards, open 'em as far as they'll go.'

'Which ain't far,' Gallant said, lying back and doing as instructed while watching with considerable misgivings as McCrae drew his gun. 'Lead hits iron, hot fragments fly, man says farewell to any thoughts of wedded bliss—'

His words were chopped short as McCrae cocked his six-gun, aimed, and pulled the trigger. Sparks danced. Metal rang. Wood splinters flew. Gunsmoke and dust drifted to reveal a chain scarred by the bullet but undamaged. McCrae swore softly, fired again; saw that the chain was still intact and pulled the trigger a third time.

With a faint clink, broken links fell apart.

Born Gallant, both hands covering his groin, grinned up at McCrae.

In that fraction of a second of mutual celebration the deputy called Madison stooped, picked up a burlap sack and flung it at Melody Lake. She had been covering the two lawmen with a small, pearl-handled revolver, but watching McCrae. The sack hit her in the face. She twisted in the saddle, flapped at the burlap with her free hand. The pistol wobbled wildly. Madison leaped out of the wagon and went for her in a dead run. Deacon snatched a shotgun from under the seat. Smoothly efficient, he cocked it, swung and lined up the weapon on McCrae's chest. His finger began whitening on the trigger.

McCrae flung himself to one side. He hit the low

sideboards hard, lost his grip on the shotgun. Still on his back, Born Gallant came up off the wagon's floor like a striking snake. With his full weight on forearms and elbows he bucked and lifted his whole lower body, twisted and snapped a kick. He caught Deacon on the side of the head. The impact was sickening. Bone would have been enough to knock the deputy cold, but it was the iron fetter encircling Gallant's right ankle that cracked against the man's temple. His eyes rolled and he went backwards out of the buckboard, shotgun flying, unconscious before he hit the hard ground. The weapon also hit the ground, butt first. The cartridge under the hammer discharged. Buckshot screamed towards the high blue skies.

'Enough!'

Madison had reached Melody before she could rip the sack from her eyes. He'd leaped up, dragged her savagely from the saddle. As she fell, he'd wrenched the pistol from her hand. Now he was levelling the small weapon at Gallant and McCrae. His teeth were bared in a snarl.

Then the horse in the buckboard's traces took over. It had begun stamping and tossing its head as behind it the action exploded. At the deafening detonation of the shotgun's barrels its eyes had widened, showing the whites, its ears had flattened. Now, as the deputy roared his warning, it squealed shrilly, reared with flashing front hoofs and bolted.

The sudden jerk as the wagon began to move knocked McCrae flat, sent Gallant sprawling. The panicked horse hit full gallop in a few long strides and headed for the bend in the trail with the buckboard rocking crazily. Gallant's horse's reins snapped tight and it was dragged alongside the buckboard, forced to gallop. McCrae's horse hesitated, ears pricked. Then Melody Lake screamed out 'Go, go, go!' and with a toss of its head the horse took off. It galloped into the dust cloud stirred up by the racing buckboard, reins flying in the wind, stirrups flapping.

Above the rattle of loose boards, the ring of iron wheel-rims on stone, the crack of the little pistol as the deputy fired futile shots that fell far, far short, Stick McCrae yelled, 'We'll have to go back, they've got Melody.'

'Melody,' Gallant said, dragging himself to his knees and clinging on for dear life, 'is in Kansas City being a lawyer – isn't that what you said?'

'Hah!'

McCrae was up on his feet. He managed two steps, moving like a drunken sailor on a ship's pitching deck. Then he fell forward, grabbed for the back of the high driver's seat and clung on. He could go no further. The rocking motion made climbing over the back impossible. The panicked horse's reins, when he leaned over and stretched one hand as far as he could, were out of reach.

'Let him be, he'll tire soon enough,' Gallant said placidly, sitting back on his heels. 'Half a mile and he'll run out of puff.'

'And stop? You're right, but those fellers'll still be too close.'

'Thought you wanted to go back?'

'Christ, all I know is it's all gone terribly wrong.'

'One of those deputies is out cold,' Gallant said, 'the other may come after us on Melody's horse, but I don't rate his chances. He's already got his back to her, figures she's nothing. If he's not careful she'll be on him like a wildcat.'

'What if you're wrong? If he's too strong for her, she'll end up in jail.'

'Fair exchange, wouldn't you say?' Gallant said, and grinned at McCrae's furious countenance as the buckboard began to slow. 'The idea was to set me free, and that's been achieved.'

'Her locked up in your place would be too high a price.' Now McCrae managed to throw a leg over the high back. He scrambled painfully, fell on to the driver's seat. By the time he'd bent and snatched at the reins the horse had pulled over to the side of the trail and stopped. It stood, lathered and trembling. Gallant's lathered gelding was pulling at the rope that tied it to the wagon, its ears flattened in fright. McCrae's horse had slowed to a trot and moved to the side of the trail, out of the thick dust, as the buckboard pulled away at breakneck speed. Only now had it caught up.

'Three horses and a wagon for the two of us,' Gallant said, dropping somewhat weakly from the buckboard and limping into the cool shade under the trees. 'They've got one horse between three of 'em.'

McCrae said nothing. He was also down out of the wagon, but had stepped into the middle of the rutted trail and was peering back the way they had come.

Gallant reckoned they'd covered a good mile, maybe more. They'd negotiated several bends, putting stands of trees and steep hillocks in the way so there'd be nothing for McCrae to see unless the deputy did indeed come after them. But if he'd acted at once, on Melody's horse he would have rapidly overtaken the slower buckboard. There was no sign of him. Gallant was thinking back, visualizing the action.

The deputy, Madison, had roared his warning and started towards the buckboard, levelling Melody's pistol. That had put Melody behind him, but there was no great need for her to stay and tangle with the tough deputy. Gallant was away and gone, her job was done, she was free to get the hell out of there.

Had she done that?

Out on the trail, McCrae was still squinting into the distance, but now shaking his head. The dust was settling. There was no movement, no sound other than the buzz of insects in the hot sun, the clink of metal as the horses moved restlessly. He walked to his patiently waiting mount, gave it an absent-minded slap on its shiny neck, then joined Gallant in the shade.

'They're forty miles from Dodge,' he said thoughtfully. 'One man's been kicked in the head with a chunk of iron, needs a doc. The only horse they've got is Melody's, the only way they can make it back is by leaving Melody and riding double.'

'Without a horse,' Gallant said, 'they could be in for a long, hard walk.'

'What d'you mean, without a horse? That second deputy. . . .'

'Madison?'

'Yes. He's still standing. He won't hesitate to take Melody's horse.'

'Madison dismissed her as no threat. Forgot about her. Stepped out on to the trail so we were in sight. Used that little popgun of hers to spit lead at us.'

A slow smile cracked McCrae's gloomy face as he remembered Melody's extraordinary capabilities.

Gallant was ahead of him.

'Before you say anything more about what we both know that gal could do to Madison,' he said, 'here's a couple of thoughts to chew on. First is that, back down the trail, a man is likely to die if left out in this heat too long. The second ties in with what we're thinking: Melody can look after herself. So what we do is turn that buckboard round now, give the horse a slap so it pulls the wagon hell for leather back down the trail.'

McCrae nodded. 'Fair enough. And Madison, if he hasn't tangled with that pretty wildcat and lost, can use it take his injured partner back to Dodge.'

FIVE

Melody Lake, bruised from the brutal fall when she was pulled from the saddle, was caught midway between her horse and the deputy, Madison, and torn with indecision.

Madison was out on the trail in the hot sun. He was standing with legs apart, his face glistening and contorted with fury. It had suddenly dawned on him that he was firing at a distant buckboard with a pistol little bigger than a gambler's derringer.

Melody couldn't decide whether to run for her horse and get the hell out of there, or tackle the deputy so she could be sure she wouldn't be pursued and he wouldn't go chasing after McCrae and Gallant. Her mind was made up in a flash when Madison suddenly swung round and she found herself gazing with horror into the small but deadly muzzle of her own pistol.

But that pistol had already been fired several times.

With a muttered curse that would have made a bartender blush she gritted her teeth and charged at the big man. A twisted root, protruding like a dead brown snake from the hard-packed earth, was her undoing. It also saved her life.

She'd run no more than ten feet when her toe caught on the root and she went down hard, rattling her teeth and stretching her length in the dust. As she did so the pistol cracked. The tiny slug whistled over her and away into the distance. Spitting dust, Melody squinted up into the sun as the deputy, with set face, again pulled the trigger. There was a harmless click.

'Hah!' Melody said. Twisting like an eel, she sprang to her feet. On the way she scooped up a fist-sized rock. Then she again charged at Madison.

But he was a powerful man, and he was thinking fast. In the seconds it took for Melody to cover the few yards separating them she saw his narrowed eyes focus on a point some way behind her. Then, almost as though absent-mindedly, he swung the hand holding the silver pistol, cracked her across the head as she closed with him, and broke into a run.

Melody staggered, but kept her feet. Her head was ringing. She could feel blood trickling down her cheek from a wound in her temple. For an instant she was seeing double. A quick shake of the head cleared her vision. At once she saw what had attracted Madison. He'd flung the silver pistol into the dust and was running for her horse.

From the boot under the right stirrup there jutted the stock of a Winchester repeating rifle.

'Oh no you don't, my boy,' Melody cried.

Planting her feet and winding up like a baseball

pitcher, she drew back her arm then hurled the rock. With a sickening crack it hit Madison's left shoulder blade. He howled in pain. Stumbling, he dropped to one knee, clutching his left arm.

Melody followed the rock. She scooped her little silver pistol out of the dust, stowed it in a pocket, took three quick paces and launched herself at the deputy. He'd dropped down by the horse and was clinging to the stirrup close to the Winchester. Landing on his back, Melody hooked her arm around his neck, wedged her forearm under his chin and dragged him several yards away from the rifle. Then she began to squeeze. All her strength was concentrated on her arm as she began strangling the deputy. At the same time, to give herself leverage, she rammed her knee into the small of his back.

Madison's body began frantically thrashing. His elbows pumped, seeking to drive hard into Melody's ribs. Desperately he tried to slip free of the arm locked around his throat. Then, unable to break her grip, he fell backwards, letting his full weight fall on Melody's slim body.

Her breath left her in a gasping whoosh. The back of Madison's head cracked against her teeth. She tasted blood as her lip split. He planted the soles of his boots on the packed earth and raised his hips from the ground. That put all his weight on his shoulders – and his broad shoulders were bearing down on Melody's chest.

I'm in a contest to see who can hold out the longest, Melody thought, ribs creaking under the strain as her

44

vision blurred. *Trouble is, the one who loses dies.* It was a frightening thought. She squeezed her eyes shut, held on. She turned her bloody face to the side as the deputy persisted in using the back of his skull as a hammer and kept her arm locked around his throat, inexorably tightening her hold. She tried with difficulty to ignore the fingers that clawed ever more weakly at her sleeve, the filthy nails that scratched at her naked wrist, and counted the dragging seconds that crawled before her closed eyes in the red haze presaging fatal darkness. Then it was over. The fingers stopped clawing. Madison's arms fell away, flopped lifelessly in the dust. His body sagged, seeming to spread its weight over Melody as the deputy lost consciousness and strength leaked from his muscles. She relaxed her right arm, let it drop from his throat, and caught herself praying that the big man wasn't dead. Then, lungs screaming for air, she desperately wriggled out from under the heavy body and lay gasping.

Recovery was swift. A few deep, shaky breaths and her strength came back with a surge. She rolled away from the inert form and climbed to her feet. Even as she did so Madison sucked in a breath, grunted something unintelligible, and his eyelids flickered. Smiling with relief, at the same time feeling justifiably smug at what she had achieved, Melody ran to her horse. She grasped the horn and reins, again gathered her strength, and thrust a foot into the stirrup.

Then she paused and looked back at the deputy who was now struggling to rise.

'Listen, feller,' she called. 'In my opinion you'd best

keep under your hat the identity of those who've made you two look stupid. Wouldn't go down too well if it got known you and Deacon have had a prisoner snatched from you by a man who pushes a pen for a living, and a woman just about tall enough for her head to reach your chin if she's wearing heeled riding boots.'

Then, allowing him a moment to think about that, and watching the sense of it register in his eyes, she swung into the saddle and spurred her eager mount away in a south-easterly direction.

That, she figured, had left an opening there if she and McCrae needed to return to Dodge. But for now the time had come – and with that realization she felt a tingle of excitement and anticipation – to put into effect the next stage of the plan she and Stick McCrae had hastily stitched together when the half-naked Born Gallant ended up in the Dodge City jail.

Yet, with the flashing hoofs beneath her pounding in concert with her racing heartbeat, the wind in her hair and the salt taste of blood fresh on her lips, she couldn't help wondering what exactly it was about the dashing blond Englishman called Born Gallant that had her, time after time, putting herself into mortal danger on his account.

SIX

'Biblical,' Stick McCrae said.

'What?'

'Your appearance. Stripped to the waist. Fettered, chained – or you have been. Body scarred from a brutal lashing, a filthy rag covering your shoulders, your blond hair unkempt, matted.'

'Conquistador,' Gallant said musingly, shifting his weight as his horse swerved to avoid a gopher hole. 'Yes, that paints a much finer picture. All the upper body armour, helmets gleaming in the sun. It's the kind of valiant image that would appeal to women.'

'Except as you are now you'd be one of the Aztecs, fleeing the advancing armies, your shoulders bowed in defeat.'

'And wet with the spittle and other bodily fluids merrily spat and expelled by cackling, contemptuous hordes,' Gallant said with a grin. 'Yes, you're right, Stick, I'm not a pleasant sight. However, defeat is a word I will never accept, and neither should you. It's thanks to you and the delightful Melody that I'm no

47

longer facing the hangman's noose.'

They'd been riding for a good ten miles from the scene of the action without much talk, not fearing pursuit but each man mulling over recent events. The attack on the buckboard had not been of Gallant's doing, and he knew the lawless actions taken by McCrae and Lake had either wrecked their careers or, perversely, given them an impressive boost that would be reflected in fame and increased salary. McCrae, for one, had a story to put into writing; he would be welcomed with open arms by any newspaper editor.

The day had started with a town marshal organizing the routine transfer of a prisoner. The move had started without a hitch, but its progress had been cut short in a few brief moments of violent conflict. Well, to be accurate, it had not been cut short. The transfer arrangements, Gallant thought with a grin, had been . . . adjusted. Instead of finishing up awaiting trial in a Kansas City cell, he would now . . . well, now what, exactly. . . ?

Gallant cocked his head and in the bright afternoon sunlight squinted across at his companion.

'By the way, Stick,' he said, 'where the hell are we going?'

'Guthrie Flint's place,' Gallant said.

In the balmy onset of a Kansas twilight they were gazing down at the splendid house backed by the barn where he, McCrae and Lake had spent one restless night during the Morton J. Slade affair. They had pulled into the woods a while ago, taking their horses from baking sunlight into welcome shade. There, he and McCrae had reached high to stretch aching muscles, then slid from their saddles. They had splashed water from canteens into their hats and used it to quench something of their mounts' thirsts, had eased cinches, then settled down with their backs against stout tree trunks to enjoy a leisurely cigarette.

Again, there had been little talk. The sun had begun its descent in the west. Comforting shade had become a blanketing darkness that brought with it necessary obscurity. The two men dozed. Eventually, rested, refreshed, they had exchanged glances, then got back into the saddle and McCrae had led the way to the fringe of the woods and silently indicated the grassy slope that led down to a meandering creek, and the house.

'You were reluctant to tell me where we were heading,' Gallant mused now, 'but this territory's painfully etched in my memory. Unbeknown to you, perhaps, I'd caught on to our destination after we'd ridden just a few miles.' He looked at the other man. 'Why the hesitation? And why here?'

'I anticipated objections. As to why here, well, where do you take an escaped murderer? That was the problem Melody and I were facing in Dodge while you snoozed in your warm cell. We were scratching our heads, flipping coins and rolling dice in the search for an answer. Flint's name came up partly out of desperation, but mostly because he's a man Melody trusts.'

'I can understand that. He helped us. But those were very different circumstances. This time we're on the wrong side of the law and, first and foremost, Guthrie's a politician.'

'And I'm a newspaperman. Flint knows that, and politicians will do anything to get their names on the front page.'

'Don't you believe it. The last thing they need is to get embroiled in dirty deeds. Bashful as spring lambs in those circs. I'm accused of killing a senator who was his close friend. On the run from the law, I'm *persona non grata*. He'll want to distance himself.'

'He'll know Slade's dead,' McCrae cut in, 'but not of your . . . well, let's just call it the part you're supposed to have played in his death. It'll be days before news of your capture and escape spreads, becomes common knowledge.'

'That may be, but d'you think I can ride down there and walk into his fancy house looking like this? I've always been raffish in appearance and habits, but right now I'm a mess.'

'Then I'll think up a story. I do it for a living.'

Gallant chuckled. 'And here's me believing you newshounds reported hard facts.'

'Dressed up to entertain. In this case it won't be difficult. Those fellers who stripped off your shirt and gave you a whipping did you a favour. When Guthrie looks at you he won't see someone who's escaped from a prison cell. Hell, you look like a raw tenderfoot who rode out West with a dream and got taken by a warring band of painted Sioux—'

'Quiet!'

Gallant had turned quickly in the saddle. Behind

them, through the trees, a dry twig had snapped. Even in open country the light was fading fast. Everywhere, long shadows appeared to be moving. Eyes and ears played tricks as a rising evening breeze rattled branches, set dry leaves rustling.

McCrae had heeded Gallant's warning. He was down, out of the saddle, using his horse as a shield between his own body and the dark woods. His drawn pistol caught the faint light, a steely glinting. Then came another sound, this time a brittle clatter, but from the same position somewhere to their rear.

Stone on stone. A dead giveaway, Gallant thought – but what kind of a man, wanting to approach with stealth, would be that careless?

Cursing softly, knowing they'd been fooled, had almost fallen for the oldest of tricks, he too slid from his horse. Unlike McCrae, he turned his back to the trees. He moved silently and with speed, drawing his six-gun as he left the saddle.

A shot boomed, the detonation that of a heavy rifle. It proved him right. The flash came from out in the open, a position fifty yards or so down the slope leading to the house, the flame belching from the muzzle dazzling in the gloom. The bullet flipped the Stetson from Stick McCrae's head, the shock of the close call rocking him forward against his horse. From several yards away Gallant heard the hiss of the bullet's flight, was almost convinced he could feel the wind of its passing. Then, as the echoes of the shot faded away across the cooling land, he heard laughter and the metallic sound of a breech being filled.

'That was a warning shot,' a harsh voice called. 'You're both outlined against what's left of the light.'

'Dark timber behind us,' Gallant answered. 'You're talking tommyrot.'

'Tell that to your friend. If either one of you makes a wrong move, the next shot takes off the top off his skull.'

A familiar voice. But where had Gallant heard it?

Thinking himself safe behind his horse, and with one hand grasping the saddle horn for steadiness, still he was inclined to believe and heed the warning. Or part of it. For now, anyway: for the few moments he would need to gather his thoughts and take stock of the situation.

But that was easy. The man with the rifle was a fool. He seemed to be alone, out in the open. McRae had been dangerously exposed but, like Gallant, had now changed his position to put his horse between him and the gunman. The advantage had tilted their way. The gunman had begun to move, riding towards them across grass damp with dew – and that was a mistake. He was now visible, even if only as a dark smudge; it was he, not they, who was outlined against the fading light.

Gallant slipped his rifle from its saddle boot. There was a whisper of sound as metal slid against leather. Then, using the cover of his horse's body to hide the movement, he backed away and slipped silently into the woods.

'Sure you know what you're doing, old boy?' he called, deliberately raising his voice to mask the metallic clack as he worked the lever that put a shell under the rifle's hammer. 'Dangerous game, don't you know, young feller like you out in the dark on his lonesome.'

'I'm paid to look after my employer's security, Gallant. What you and your pard are doing is acting suspicious on Flint land.'

By George, he knows me, and I should know him, Gallant thought. *Still can't place him, more's the pity – but the fact that he knows me makes this situation much more dangerous.*

'Can't argue with the bit about trespassing on Flint's land,' he said, 'but why suspicious? We're riders resting after a long day in the saddle, easing tired muscles and stiff limbs, don't you know?'

The rider had reined in his horse. In the brief time since the shot had been fired, the light had almost gone. Even though the gunman was much closer, Gallant could still see little more than the outline of a horse, the rider's shape, the outline of a Stetson. It was enough. Down on one knee, he lifted the rifle, snugged the butt into the hollow of his shoulder.

Several yards away to his right, McCrae's eyes glinted as he caught the movement and turned his head towards Gallant. He saw the lifted rifle, the cheek pushed hard into the worn wooden stock as Gallant became still and took careful aim.

'You're playing a dangerous game,' McCrae called, deliberately drawing attention his way to give Gallant the few seconds he needed to get settled. 'Throwing a stone over our heads, using a couple of cheap tricks that wouldn't deceive—'

'Oh, you were deceived all right,' the gunman cut in, 'and if there's anyone playing dangerous games it surely ain't me.'

Even as he spoke, behind Gallant and McCrae three shots blasted, so close together as to sound like one. These were the lighter cracks of a handgun. The muzzle flashes lit up the thick tree trunks, the canopy of leaves. This time Gallant was the target. In the darkness, aiming was guesswork and the bullets went too low. Or maybe that was the intention. One clipped his boot, ripped away the heel. The powerful side force on his leg twisted him off balance. He fell heavily, making the brush crackle, thorns in the undergrowth tearing at his naked skin as the filthy blanket was torn from his body.

Then came two more shots, again from behind but from a different direction. Gallant cursed softly. He and McCrae were victims of a clever double bluff. Men deep in the woods had deliberately snapped twigs and knocked stone against stone to make it appear that the man riding in across open ground was playing tricks. He listened to the snick of branches as bullets hissed through the trees over McCrae's head. Heard a rustling as leaves fell in a shower, followed by the unmistakable sound of a body falling into undergrowth.

Gallant was struggling to rise. What had he heard? McCrae diving for cover, or going down with a bullet through his head? He was back on his knees, using the rifle as a stick to help him up, when a man came charging through the trees like a crazed steer and took him from behind. The heavy body knocked Gallant flat, drove the breath from his body. He was down, on his back. Above him, against the night sky, a hand rose high. It came swinging down, carrying the glint of heavy metal. Desperately, Gallant twisted, felt the six-gun take the skin from his shoulder. He whipped his left hand upwards and sideways in a vicious chopping blow. Its edge connected with the soft flesh under an unshaven chin, the bulge of an Adam's apple. The man choked, rolled away. Gallant bent his knees, kicked with both feet, again he connected. This time it was with a hard body, a midriff, and he heard the whoosh of a man's expelled breath.

Away to his right there were sounds of a fierce struggle: knuckles hitting hard bone, grunts of effort, gasps of pain. McCrae was alive, but fighting for his life against a second man who had come silently through the woods to take them from behind. Then, as Gallant again bemoaned his stupidity, he heard the crackle of brush as a third gunman came through the undergrowth, deliberate, unhurried, sure of what he was doing.

It was the last thing Gallant heard. Even as he saw the man he had punched in the throat come to his knees, begin to lift his six-gun, a mighty blow crashed down on his skull and he floated away into redness and oblivion.

SEVEN

Gallant was vaguely aware of being thrown bodily across a horse, then of a short but painful ride downhill, belly down, head and legs hanging and a saddle horn digging like a hard fist into his middle. The scent of gunsmoke was in his nostrils, then a fresher, cleaner smell as the sharp hoofs of several horses cut into wet grass and through to the rich soil. Then they thudded on harder ground, the deep voice of a man calling questions; a wait, followed by more talk, and then the sound of riders leaving, the rattle of hoofs fading into the night stillness.

Then, once more, Born Gallant drifted into unconsciousness.

He regained his senses lying on his side on dry, packed earth. His eyes flicked open. At once, he recognized his surroundings: the inside of a barn, one that was hauntingly familiar. Now, with the return of consciousness, the scent was of straw, of horse ordure, of hemp and timber, the faint smell of hot coal oil from a lamp dimly lighting the barn's spacious interior. For an instant he expected to see Melody Lake sashaying towards him in the swishing low-cut dress favoured by dance-hall girls, but that of course was a flicker of memory from several months back, the dress had then been a disguise; now the woman herself was . . . well, just where was Melody Lake?

'Gallant's coming to. He'll be able to confirm what I just told you. About a saloon owner called Eamon Brannigan, the use of a whip to exact revenge for what went on at Buck Creek, and the killing of those evil sons of his, Sean and Patrick.'

The words shimmered in Gallant's ears, coming and going. Lying with his back to the speaker, he allowed himself a thin, hidden smile. Stick McCrae was intelligently alerting Gallant to what had been said, to the pure fiction he had fed to. . . ? Well, to Guthrie Flint, of course. This was Flint's barn, his house was across the yard, his had been the gruff voice asking questions as Gallant was borne across the yard belly-down.

Gallant rolled over. As if he had just awoken from a refreshing night's sleep he clambered shakily to his feet, yawned, then grinned apologetically as his boot's missing heel caused him to stagger like a late-night drunk.

'Damned rude, I know, but what can a man do when he's as jaded as I feel. Must say it's super to see you again, Flint. You're looking chipper, too. Sound in wind and limb, what?'

'Cut it out, Gallant,' the big politician said roughly.

'Playing the fool won't work with me. By the looks of you it didn't work with this Eamon Brannigan. Don't know the man, don't approve of his methods, but the death of even one son can blur the difference between right and wrong.'

'And now it's my turn to say cut it out,' Gallant retorted. 'As far as *I* recall it was *you* telling me – a few months back – that it was the Brannigan boys who were robbing that Dodge bank when Senator Slade's young son Jericho took a bullet; *you* telling me the Brannigans were holed up at the Travis spread.'

'I have too many important matters occupying my mind to be bothered with irrelevancies,' Flint snapped dismissively.

He swung away, paced across the hard ground, then he turned; as he came back again his eyes never left Gallant. A big fat cigar held between his podgy fingers trailed aromatic blue smoke. He was even bigger than Gallant remembered. A huge paunch caused the white shirt to bulge under the open jacket of a black serge suit. A gunbelt drooping beneath the distended belly held an ivory-handled engraved six-gun. He had lost some of his grizzled grey hair and, what seemed most unexpected to Gallant, was now openly hostile. On their previous meetings he had praised Gallant's exploits when working for the Pinkertons. Now. . . ? Well, Gallant thought, watching him strut, he and McCrae were in the echoing barn, not being plied with drink in the comfort of the house. Didn't that speak volumes?

As for McCrae, alive he might be, but he had been

well marked in the struggle up in the woods. One eye was swollen shut and turning purple. He was standing awkwardly, which suggested that hard blows or kicks to the body had cracked one or more ribs. On his right thigh his six-gun's leather holster hung empty. Gallant had already established that his own six-gun had been taken; he was now unarmed, and if vision and hearing were anything to go by he was almost certainly suffering from a mild concussion.

'I suppose one of those important, relevant matters,' Gallant said, 'is figuring out what to do with me.'

Flint stopped abruptly, stabbed at Gallant with the cigar.

'That's already been decided and acted upon.'

From the shadows a voice said, 'Riders are on their way to Kansas City. When they return, the town's marshal will be with them. You've got an appointment with the gallows, Gallant.'

McCrae had turned quickly. He said, 'You a part of this? I thought we were friends?'

'Work pards, Stick. Now not even that.'

A tall man wearing a black Stetson so old it was turning green came away from the stacked straw bales where he'd been standing, out of the lamplight. His whole outfit was black and faded, the six-gun in its tied-down holster no doubt just as old, but its walnut butt had been polished to a high shine by use. Gallant nodded slowly, recognizing the man, mentally visualizing a sequence of events that had led from a Wichita saloon to the woods south of Dodge City, and now to this confrontation in Guthrie Flint's barn.

'Chet Eagan,' Gallant said, grimacing. 'I guess I talked too much in the Buckhorn, Eagan; told you where I was heading. What did you do? Ride ahead to Dodge, pass on the good news to Brannigan?'

Even as he kept up McCrae's fictitious story about a Brannigan involvement Gallant was turning angrily to indicate the striped skin of his naked back. 'If you did, then you'll pay' – the look in Gallant's blue eyes was chilling – 'but you must have ridden your poor nag into the ground getting back here from Dodge to tell Flint of my arrest, and I don't understand why.'

'Eagan works for me,' Flint said, 'keeps me up to date with events that might be of interest to a man in my position.'

Gallant shook his head in disbelief. 'I'm flattered I fall into that category. But I was being taken to Kansas City for trial. How did Eagan know I'd escaped?'

'I didn't,' Eagan said, moving in to stand alongside Flint. 'You and McCrae were spotted up there in the trees. Not identified until later, but smoking too many cigarettes gave away your position. I keep my eyes open. When daylight fades a struck match flares like a beacon.'

Flint gestured impatiently at Gallant with his cigar. 'Another irrelevancy. Doesn't matter where or how you were apprehended. For murdering my close friend, Morton Slade, you'll hang by the neck until very dead. And that saddens me. Until recently I had you down as a decent man.'

'I dumped the killer of Slade's son at his feet, and

he was grateful to the point of tears, shook my hand with both of his when I left. If I did change, become a cold-blooded killer, why would I go after Morton Slade?

'That could be one of life's mysteries,' Flint said, 'but right now we're done talking. McCrae, I'll take you over to the house. We'll share good food and drink, discuss the newspaper business and how your involvement in it can help me. Eagan, make Gallant secure in here, then get yourself something to eat—'

He broke off as a rifle cracked and between his feet a bullet kicked up dirt. The violent detonation sent a roosting bird fluttering wildly from the barn's high rafters, and brought down dust that caught at the throat and dispersed to become a myriad motes floating in the lamp's dim glow.

In the ensuing deathly stillness the challenging question came in a cool, feminine voice that rang loud and clear, rising and echoing.

'D'you think for one minute it's going to be that easy?'

Flint didn't turn. The only signs that he had heard the mocking words or been startled by the bullet was a slight narrowing of the eyes, and a sudden crisp tearing sound as his fingers tightened and crushed the cigar's leaves.

Alongside him Chet Egan spun round fast. Standing bow-taut, he dropped his right hand to his six-gun. Then, seeing what he was up against, he froze with his fingertips brushing the butt and an obscene curse falling from lips drawn back in a snarl.

McCrae, clearly, had been watching the barn's big, open doorway, without once allowing his posture to give anything away. Now, finding difficulty suppressing a grin, he flashed a hard glance at Gallant and made a spreading gesture with both hands held low. In the sudden silence, taking advantage of the shock that had turned Flint and Egan to stone men with gazes averted, he and Gallant began to move stealthily towards either side of the barn.

'Melody Lake,' Guthrie Flint said softly. Now he did turn round, moving lightly for a big man; his eyes fixed on the dark-haired young woman and took careful note of the way she leaned casually in the doorway while managing to cover the politician and Eagan with her Winchester rifle.

'I notice a cut lip,' Flint said, 'and bloodstains on your shirt. Also, I'm quite sure I can see an unnatural swelling on your temple. You've been in the wars, my dear, which perhaps explains your unnecessary and very careless handling of that dangerous weapon. But tell me, what on earth brings you here?'

'It was a plan, spawned out of desperation. You helped us once before when we were in trouble, so it was natural we should turn to you again. But from what I've heard, I'd say you've got several screws loose. Born Gallant a cold-blooded killer? Your brains are addled, Flint.'

'That's as maybe, but there was a witness to the crime and that seems to remove any doubt. Gallant will be tried, but a guilty verdict is inevitable.'

'Gallant's a long way from any courtroom,' Lake

said bluntly, 'and I'm impatient. Back off and unbuckle your gunbelt, Flint. You – Eagan is it? – do exactly the same, then take off your filthy vest and shirt and toss them in Gallant's direction.'

'Not sure if I'm entirely in favour of that last bit, don't you know,' Gallant said, making his disgust evident as he stared at Eagan's trail- and sweat-stained garments. But he was again playing the fool, and doing it with intent. Misdirected, Guthrie Flint's eyes followed the direction of Gallant's lip-curling, disdainful gaze. In that instant Gallant launched himself at the politician.

His naked shoulder slammed into the big man's bulging midriff. He heard the breath gust from a suddenly gaping mouth, felt fat fingers holding the crumbled remnants of a cigar scrabble futilely at his face. Driving through with all the power of his legs, he grabbed a handful of shirt in his fist and followed the politician down. They hit the dirt floor with Gallant on top, using his weight. He heard the crack of a skull against the hard ground, saw Flint's eyes glaze, and quickly he cast a glance towards Chet Eagan.

The one-time newspaperman was giving a creditable performance as a fighting gunslinger. He'd sprung into action as soon as Gallant made his move. Like Gallant, he took advantage of misdirection. Both Stick McCrae and Melody Lake had instinctively followed Gallant's attack on the politician. Their heads and eyes were still turned in that direction when Eagan leaped at McCrae.

His fist cracked against the Dodge City man's jaw.

McCrae had already taken a beating in the woods. Now his legs began to buckle. Eagan grabbed him from behind. He slipped his left arm under McCrae's arms and around his chest. Holding him up, he swung him so that the dazed man was facing Melody Lake. Then, clean and fast, Eagan drew his six-gun. He thrust it under McCrae's arm and levelled it at the young woman.

'Drop the rifle,' he said, the softness of his delivery adding to the aura of menace.

'Mexican stand-off,' Lake said coolly, and she waggled the rifle's barrel. 'Shoot me, Eagan, and before I die I'll put a slug clean through Flint's ugly head.'

'You'd risk hitting Gallant.'

'Don't put money on it,' Gallant said. He kept his weight bearing down, grabbed the groaning politician by what was left of his hair and twisted his white, glistening face towards Lake. 'Well-oiled team, working together, don't you know. The young lady with the Winchester can now line her sights on this confirmed whiskey-drinker's red nose, impossible to miss.'

The nonsensical talk was again meant to distract. Gallant had hardly finished babbling when McCrae clamped his arm on Eagan's gun hand and simply fell over. He dragged Eagan down with him. Before they'd hit the dirt floor, Gallant had sprung off Flint. He whacked the politician in the face with the side of his closed fist as he rose, took two long strides and kicked Eagan in the face. The six-gun skittered across the floor. Eagan collapsed like a punctured balloon, his eyes rolling horribly to reveal the whites.

Melody Lake was shaking her head as she came away from the door.

'Marquis of Queensbury rules, Gallant. That ring a bell?'

'Welsh feller called Chambers wrote 'em, the ninth Marquis, John Douglas, endorsed 'em,' Gallant said.

'And you just broke the one that has to do with hitting a man when he's down.'

'Not in my list,' Gallant said. 'English aristocrats make their own rules, keep them a jealously guarded secret to confuse the peasants.'

'You're beginning to annoy me,' Lake said, 'but leaving that to be settled later, what do we do now?'

'Run, hide, do some thinking,' McCrae croaked. 'Coming here for help was the plan. It's not worked out.'

'Never could, never would,' Flint growled.

He had rolled over. Rubbing his jaw, he'd somehow made it to his feet. Now he was glowering at them, thin hair unkempt, eyes ugly. 'My advice is give yourselves up to the law. Can't see that doing much for you, Gallant.'

'Which rules it out as an option, wouldn't you say?' Gallant rubbed his naked shoulders, shivered, looked at McCrae. 'Eagan's still down and out. Are you fit enough to stay here and watch over him? No, better still, find some rope and tie his wrists and ankles. I'm in need of clothes.' He turned to Flint. 'You had a son called Billie who was about my size—'

'You bastard—'

'—and my guess is you've kept his room like a shrine, untouched, underwear in drawers, outer garments in fine oak wardrobes. He was your only son – right?'

Flint glared, nodded.

'Well, call me a bastard if you will, but you know I did what I could to help him and now it's his turn. But what about your wife? Seem to recall last time I was here you mentioned a fair-haired woman?'

'My second wife,' Flint said, mustering some dignity, perhaps using his politician's skill to draw sympathy. 'Billie's mother died some years ago. Sadly, it seems I'm destined to die a widower, for my second wife's beautiful hair turned grey, and she too passed away.'

'I'm sorry to hear that,' Gallant said, not for one second taken in by the false grief. 'Melody, let's you and me help this tired old man over to his house so he can fall into bed. You've been in there, know where he keeps the strong drink, and you can rattle decanter and glasses while I drape garments over the frame to hide the scars.'

'Adding theft to murder,' Flint said.

'Working backwards, from major crime to misdemeanour,' Gallant said wryly. 'Go back far enough and I'll wind up innocent. But talk's becoming dangerous, because it takes time we haven't got. Stick, follow us over to the house when Eagan's trussed. And make it snappy. We leave it too long before we put this place behind us, Eagan's pards will be back from Kansas City with men wearing badges.'

EIGHT

The cold hours that come before a chill dawn are not the best of times for the bruised, battered and concussed to look for refuge, and when faced with that problem it's natural for the mind to seek the familiar. When Gallant had been hunting for the killers of the late Senator Morton J. Slade's young son, he had been told by an obliging Guthrie Flint that the place thought to be used by them as a hideout was a rundown ranch known as the Travis spread. It lay some way to the west of Wichita, and could be located by using a landmark known as Lone Cree Ridge. Further to the West was the small town of Buck Creek – but Gallant had no intention of returning there to tangle with the tough Irish saloon keeper known as Eamon Brannigan. Unless, of course, it was that ruffian who had been behind the whipping, and that remained to be seen.

Back then they had found their way to the Travis spread. It had gone up in flames when one of the desperate outlaws Gallant and McCrae had violently confronted had deliberately thrown a lighted oil lamp into a passageway. As was intended, it had shattered, and the fire that began licking at the walls had almost destroyed the buildings. But in Gallant's opinion, that made what was left of the spread ideal as a temporary hideout. A quick look at the place would tell any posse sent out to hunt him down that it was uninhabitable – but there were outbuildings far enough away from the house to have escaped the flames, and almost hidden in thick woods.

Once they'd discussed the idea briefly and quickly agreed on the destination, they left Flint's house in a hurry. They stopped only long enough for Melody Lake to see to McCrae's wounds, to take enough food from the big pantry to keep them going for some days and for which Gallant paid with silver. Gallant took what he needed from the younger Flint's room: clean denim trousers, laundered underwear and shirts, a worn leather vest, a Stetson that had been carelessly tossed on the floor near the bed with expensive boots that were not Gallant's size and could not in any case have been slipped on over the iron fetters.

Finally, and most important, he and McCrae had armed themselves; the limping McCrae found a six-gun and ammunition in a cupboard in a back room; an apologetic but crookedly smiling Gallant demanded and got the politician's gunbelt and engraved Colt pistol.

Guthrie Flint watched them impassively, knocking back imported Scotch whisky to dull the ache of a pounding head, every so often glancing from the window towards the barn where somewhere in the darkness Chet Eagan lay bound and gagged. He all but ignored them when they left, merely glaring balefully, and the last they saw of the politician was his bulky figure looming large against the lamplight in the house's big front window.

'Used to be a friend, now he's an enemy,' Melody Lake said. 'The double-crossing sonofabitch.'

'Unladylike language, but you're right, and he's a dangerous enemy with too much influence for comfort,' Born Gallant said over his shoulder. He presented a familiar lean figure in unfamiliar clothing; beneath the Stetson his long blond hair was blowing in the wind. 'But, hell, we're in so deep, in my book adding one more enemy just makes the game more interesting.'

'You English,' McCrae said, 'seem to have trouble distinguishing play from the really serious stuff.' With a shake of the head he spurred away into the night.

'The only way I can see of getting close to the identity of the big man who had me hung from a tree by the wrists is to talk to that new marshal, Cole Banning. Trouble is, if we show our faces in Dodge City we'll end up staring at strips of sunlight from the inside of the calaboose.'

Gallant looked at the others for confirmation. He was seated on a log, his strong white teeth tearing at ham cooked over a wood fire and now and then washing down the tough meat with strong black coffee. Smoke from the fire drifted, mingling with the white early-morning mist that blanketed the grassland surrounding the Travis spread. To Gallant, the smell of that wood fire was indistinguishable from the lingering stink of the inferno that had destroyed the buildings. He had the queasy feeling that time was shifting, that past and present were becoming so close and intermingled that it was impossible to tell them apart. . . .

'Gloom and doom are not in your character, so snap out of it,' Melody Lake said, jerking Gallant from his reverie. 'Besides, I can assure you things are not as bad as they seem.'

'Oh yeah, so what was it you did to that deputy, Madison?' Stick McCrae cut in caustically. 'He suffered the indignity of being choked half to death by a feisty young woman lawyer, and as far as we know Gallant killed Deacon with a single blow from the iron he's still carrying on his ankles. OK, all I did was hold up two lawmen with a shotgun – hah! – and that's all I did! But you think they're going to let us walk free?'

'But don't you see?' Melody said. 'It's that indignity you mentioned that's going to work for us.'

Gallant, flushed from the heat of the fire, caught on immediately.

'They'll keep quiet to save face, you mean?' he said. 'Or make up a story, tell Banning they were overpowered by a gang of toughs, something like that?' He cocked his head, greasy bacon poised on the point of his knife.

'It's the advice hidden not too deeply in the hint I gave Madison,' Melody said, smiling primly. 'The keeping quiet bit, I mean.'

'And, by George, I do believe he'll follow it,' Gallant said. 'But even then I'm ruled out from going there. I'm the dangerous escaped prisoner, sure to be spotted. Alarm raised, bugles blowing and all that – end of story. That means it's down to one of you.'

'Or both,' Melody said.

'Yes, why not,' Gallant said, raising an eyebrow at McCrae. 'But are you up to it? You've got an eye like a purple plum. Your brain was rattled about in your skull, your jaw took a nasty crack.' He shook his head. 'And you, Melody, bruised and cut. . . .'

'But only my appearance has been altered, or you'd still be in that barn being mistreated by the awful Guthrie Flint.'

'True,' Gallant said. 'And I admire your pluck. So, both of you ride in. Couple of brash journalists stamping into Banning's office to pick his brains, that's something he'd expect.'

'But where will it get us?' McCrae asked shrewdly. 'OK, we might come up with the name of the man who hung you from the bough of a tree like a bloody side of beef. And maybe you can go find him. But you'll still be left accused of the murder of a state senator.'

'About which you will attempt to learn more when talking to Cole Banning. The more we know, the more strings to our bow. Or bows.'

'And where will you be?' Melody said.

'The seriously bruised skin around my delicate ankles tells me I should sneak into Dodge by a circuitous route and pay that bearded blacksmith a visit.'

'He's a maker not a breaker, and another man mightily averse to losing face,' Melody said. 'We'll watch for sparks flying over the iron roofs, then ride like hell in the opposite direction.'

'With friends like you two,' Gallant said, grinning, 'who needs enemies?'

NINE

If Melody Lake had been asked to describe Marshal Cole Banning in one word, she would at once have chosen laconic. Or perhaps taciturn. Or were they the same? Well, she was by training a lawyer not a journalist, but she knew roughly what both meant and so she wasn't too surprised when the taciturn or laconic lawman hit her with a no-nonsense question as she walked into the jail office.

'Where have you been?'

'Been?' Melody looked suitably confused. 'Been nowhere, and now I'm here.'

'Tom says you and McCrae have been missing most of yesterday and all of today.'

'Yes, well, my editor knows we're newshounds with his business interests at heart. We've been out chasing the Born Gallant story.'

'Looks like you ran into some trouble.' Banning touched his forehead, his lip. 'Bruises and cuts. What happened?'

'Fell off my horse,' Melody said, deadpan. 'Took a short cut, low branch nearly took my head off. I split my lip trying to kiss the hard ground.'

'And the scrub scratched you some on the way down.' He touched his wrist, and Melody knew he'd noticed the damage done by Madison's nails.

There was silence for a moment as Banning watched her. His lips were pursed, his eyes registering disbelief. 'So, chasing the Gallant story how? Gallant's on his way to Kansas City under guard. Trial and conviction, followed by hanging. There is no story.'

'Goodness. Well, it seems our chasing was all for nothing; we could have come here and got the information straight from . . . from the horse's mouth.'

'But as you just said, you are here.' Banning was seated at his desk, feet up, smoking a cigarette that was mostly brown paper. 'Why?'

'Laconic as hell,' Melody muttered under her breath. Then she strode away from the sunlight streaming in the door, sat elegantly on a straight-backed chair and tried swiftly to gather her thoughts.

Clearly, something wasn't right. Discussing the two injured deputies, she had suggested to Gallant and McCrae that they would limp back into Banning's office and tell him they'd been overpowered by a gang out to free the Englishman. But from what Banning had just said, he was unaware that Gallant had escaped. That meant the deputies had not yet returned to Dodge City. They had the buckboard, so where were they? What were they doing?

She was aware of Banning watching her, waiting for

an answer.

'When one story finishes, another begins,' she said. 'Gallant may be heading for a necktie party, but he was flogged with a whip before his arrest. You know that. You saw him, had him cut down. According to what McCrae was told at the scene, the man responsible had grey-streaked hair to his shoulders, a face carved from stone and unnaturally blue eyes. Rode a thoroughbred chestnut gelding a simple town marshal like you could never afford.'

'Ignoring the insult, and looking back at what happened with common sense, whoever he is he did the law a favour: he kept a tight hold on Gallant until I got there. The fact that he made him feel some pain while waiting might actually please some folk, and here I'm thinking particularly of a certain senator's good wife.'

Homing in on the point of relevance to her visit, Melody said, 'Whoever he is? Does that mean you don't recognize my description of that man?'

'Stone-face, long hair, pale eyes, beating the hell out of Gallant? To me that sounds like a gunslinger come riding out of that man's past, bearing a grudge.'

'Gallant doesn't have much of a past in this country. And can you see a gunslinger on a thoroughbred horse?'

'Stolen.'

There was a leaden pause. Cigarette smoke curled in the shafts of sunlight. Melody could feel the pulse in her throat, the sudden impulse to slap this man's face. She breathed deeply and smiled sweetly.

'Putting to one side the nonsense of a gunslinger

riding a stolen horse, what about the case against Born Gallant?'

'Out of my hands.'

'You're saying nothing?'

'Ask me if I trust journalists.' He waited. Melody let him wait. Banning shrugged. 'You're too late. Gallant's finished. If you must chase the impossible, then you should talk to the Jehu who was driving Senator Slade's stagecoach as if all the demons in hell were after him. Name's Coleman. I can tell you where to find him.'

'Do that,' Melody said, and a bright smile lit up her face. Hell, two could play the laconic game, and at least she'd got something.

Born Gallant rode boldly through the back alleys of Dodge City with his blond hair tucked up under the borrowed Stetson and wearing clothes that, if they identified him at all, would make people look twice and still not believe their eyes. *Billie Flint had died, shot in the back in woods to the south, they'd say later, but I'll be damned if I didn't see him – or his ghost – sneaking back into town.*

Well, that sense of *dis*belief was part of what Gallant was relying on. The other bit was his belief that a burly bearded blacksmith had for some reason winked at him after cruelly locking his ankles in hand-made fetters. With it had come the growing certainty that there was something about the blacksmith that was hauntingly familiar.

He found his way to the smithy without difficulty.

Used nose and eyes, he thought, grinning. Those senses took him to the run-down shack well away from the centre of Dodge. Above it a hazy pall of smoke added a dirty grey to cloudless blue skies, and the smell of hot metal strongly reminded Gallant of the heavy iron fetters still chafing his raw ankles.

Inside the shack the forge itself was the centrepiece that dominated, a big rectangular iron container in which heaped charcoal was, in places, almost white-hot and sent light and heat bouncing back from rotting timber walls. The blacksmith had his back to Gallant. He was standing in front of another deep container up against a side wall, which Gallant knew was filled with water used to quench hot metal: tempering the steel of manufactured knife-blades, or simply cooling an item so that the blacksmith could clutch it with his bare hands.

'Expected you,' the man growled, not turning. 'Thought you'd've been quicker, but didn't take into account that you're English.'

'Don't think that's a compliment,' Gallant remarked, 'so I'll treat it as an insult, but let it slide 'cause I need your primitive skills.' Now the huge blacksmith did turn. He was naked to the waist, his hairy chest and belly shielded from sparks and flame by a scarred, full-length leather apron. He was holding a horseshoe in a hand that made the curved metal look like a child's toy. His face was impassive, but above what was mostly a tangle of black beard his dark eyes were shining with what Gallant was unsurprised to observe was good humour.

'Didn't say a word coming in, so how'd you know it was me?'

'McCrae came to me, said he needed a horse in a hurry. He already had a fine specimen he was riding. You were on your way to Kansas City, and knowing you were a friend of his made it easy to work out his intentions.' The blacksmith shrugged. 'I told him your gelding was in Jake's barn. Every horse has a distinctive gait.'

'You use big words for a feller works with his hands.' Gallant watched the big man toss the horseshoe away, sending it clinking on to a pile heaped on sacking. 'You recognized the horse, got confirmation from the clanking of the severed chains on my fetters. That explains you, but something's nagging at me, telling me I should recognize you when common sense tells me that's impossible.'

'Big words is the clue.'

Gallant raised an eyebrow.

'Big words, big names,' the blacksmith hinted. 'Mine's Theodore, so take an initial step back in the alphabet—'

'Glory be!' Gallant said, mentally kicking himself. 'T backwards to S leads me to a man driving a freighter, a bearded muleskinner who helped me when I was figuring out how to snatch Billie Flint from the jaws of death. You're Sebastian Bullock's brother.'

'His twin.'

'Identical,' Gallant said, 'and I couldn't see it.'

'Give yourself a break. On your way to a date with the hangman, all you saw was a sweaty brute bending iron strips around your ankles.'

'And winking at me,' Gallant mused. 'Wondered about that, could have had me worried.'

Theodore Bullock glowered. 'Don't push your luck, Gallant. Taking those fetters off can be easy or hard – and I mean for you, not me.'

With a spring in his step and a song in his heart, Born Gallant danced a jig around the fierce red heat of the iron forge and for the first time in two days his movements caused no clinking of metal chains. Theodore Bullock had twisted the fetters from his ankles using long-handled iron bolt cutters powerful enough to clamp on and bend the tracks of the railroad running through the centre of Dodge. He'd done it without causing pain, with the bedside manner of a country doctor and the tenderness of a doctor's wife. Or maybe not the latter, Gallant thought, recalling the grim wives of doctors he had known during his army days.

He chuckled, and came to a halt, breathless.

Bullock was watching him impassively. He was slumped easily on a three-legged wooden stool against one of the sagging board walls, drinking whiskey straight from the bottle. What could be seen of his face above the beard was red from exertion and the glow of the forge. Through the wide-open doors, Gallant's horse had been watching the merry capering with nervous eyes and with ears pricked.

'Took a big risk, coming here,' Gallant said, stepping across and plucking the bottle from the

79

blacksmith's filthy hand. 'Always possible you'd take one look at me, slug me unconscious and carry me across your shoulder like a dead rabbit to Banning's jail.'

'Sebastian was in town, day you got brung in after that whipping and thrown in jail. We talked in here,' Bullock pointed at the bottle, 'did some drinking, it being conducive to thought.' Startlingly white teeth flashed in a whiskery grin. 'Truth is, after what you did for Billie Flint you can do no wrong in Seb's eyes. I trust his judgement. Case of having to: if I went against him it'd be me out cold, not you. Anyhow, he's out hauling freight not too far from here, but keeping his eyes and ears open. Does his share of hard drinking, as you'll have gathered, and there's nowhere better for picking up loose talk than a saloon bar around closing time.'

'Decent of him,' Gallant said, wiping the neck of the bottle with his palm and tossing it back to be caught deftly. 'Trouble is, there was a witness saw me at the scene of the crime.'

'Distinctive features make a man easy to recognize,' Bullock said. 'Or impersonate. Both us Bullocks are bigger than most men, with beards like black bushes. I've more than once been taken for Seb.'

'With me it's fair hair, and a silly way of talking,' Gallant said ruefully. 'That last bit's a deliberate affectation which at times proves useful, but I see what you're getting at. Any towhead with evil intentions and an ear for dialect could pass himself off as me. Knowing that is the easy bit. Locating this thespian killer who was sent out to get me accused of murder will prove more difficult.'

Bullock's eyes were thoughtful. 'It was my suggestion, but is that what you believe? One man doing another's dirty work for cash payment?'

'Thinking along those lines, yes.'

'Hired killer, in and out. Looks like you, talks like you, and then he doesn't. Difficult to find. Better to go after the payer. Start thinking about whose nose you could've put out of joint.'

'The list is long, though not many of those on it would stoop to murder. And believe me, my friend, the murder is what's driving me. Leaving aside my various physical and mental injuries and the nasty shadow of the noose, Senator Morton J. Slade became a good friend for whom I once sweated blood. We'll find the swine who killed him, and the search has already begun. While I'm chewing the fat with you, my trusty scouts are out riding the range in their search for truth.'

'General Custer, risen from the dead and back from the Little Big Horn,' Bullock said, rolling his eyes. 'Incidentally, how's the back?'

'Good as new – almost. Borrowed clothes are a bit rough on skin that's still sensitive, but I'm a fast healer.'

Now, with the torment Gallant had suffered brought to the fore, Bullock's black eyes held a warning.

'Melody Lake's a sweet kid, Gallant, and as feisty as they come. Asking questions is what she does well, because she's a lawyer-cum-journalist, but when it comes to the rough stuff you want to keep her well clear.'

'That,' Gallant said, rising and leaning over to shake the blacksmith's hand before taking his leave, 'would be like trying to keep the fox away from the chicken coop, or the cat from licking the jug of cream. . . .'

He broke off. Bullock's eyes had narrowed. The big frame stiffened, the bottle clattered to the floor. A brawny palm reached back to push his bulk away from the wall, and he got his legs under him as the startled Gallant swung around. Then both of them stopped moving.

Deputy Madison had stepped silently into the gloom of the smithy. The sun was at his back, making him loom large. He had a six-gun in his hand.

'Sensible,' the lawman said, 'so let's keep it like that.' The weapon never wavered as he circled the small workshop, putting the glowing forge between him and the two men.

His voice sounded hoarse. *His throat's hurting*, Gallant thought, and wondered why.

The blacksmith was livid.

'Who the hell are you to call me sensible?'

'Shut up, and stay where you are, Bullock, you've done enough damage taking off those irons. Gallant, use your aristocratic English fingers to lift that fancy six-gun and drop it on the floor. Your taste of freedom's over. That journey to the gallows is about to start all over again. This time you'll make it – and it don't much matter if you're alive or dead.'

TEN

Although the plan had been for him to go with Melody to talk to Marshal Cole Banning, Stick McCrae had reasoned that two people doing the one job was a sheer waste of ears and eyes. On the ride in to Dodge they had tossed around several ideas: ways in which Stick could make himself useful. There was a desperate need for information to help Gallant. Information was their business. The man who ran their business was Tom Caton. Tom was the editor of the *Dodge City Times.*

When McCrae had tied his horse, climbed the rickety outside stairs and walked into the dusty office above the big room housing the printing presses, Caton didn't look up. A perspiring fat man wearing a green eyeshade over wire spectacles, a limp white shirt with steel armbands holding his sleeves, he was sitting behind a desk littered with paper. All of it was ink-stained. A prominent spike pierced crumpled news-story rejects.

'You're fired,' Caton snapped, and licked a pencil.

McCrae slumped into a chair. 'That's the third time this week.'

'So what are you doing here?'

'You need me.'

'Like I need a bullet in the head.'

'The presses are silent.'

'Mid-week they're always silent.'

'And they'll stay that way, because without a story there's nothing to print.'

'And I suppose you've got one,' Caton said, and now he looked up. 'What happened to your eye?'

'A drunk mistook me for his mother-in-law.'

'Hah! OK, back to something that's printable. What, and when?'

'By the end of the week. The Gallant story.'

'Dawn on Saturday, Gallant will be a dead man. Dodge City's weary of dead men. Trigger-happy Texans stinking of cattle sprayed the town with hot lead. The citizens of Dodge City are up to their ears in dead men.'

'Born Gallant's no killer. If I can prove that, he'll walk free and the United States President will be reading your newspaper in his Washington office.'

Caton stared, thought some, and sighed. He flung down his pencil and sat back.

'If that's so, then shouldn't you be out there getting that proof?'

'An eyewitness to the senator's murder is sending Gallant to the gallows. If I can discredit the witness. . . .'

'Knock a manufactured story on the head, open the

way to truth and light – that what you mean?' Caton nodded, suddenly intent, thoughtful. 'But you're here, giving me a hard time. Why? Am I supposed to know something?'

'Not something. You know everything,' McCrae said, 'because that's your job.' He grinned. 'You know Stan Coleman, the driver of the stagecoach, the eyewitness. So tell me about him. Give me something I can use.'

For a moment Caton was silent. Then he gestured vaguely.

'The reliance put on what Coleman said in his statement has been . . . troubling me.'

'Seventy years old, but the eyes and ears of a man of fifty, honest all his life. His evidence cannot be doubted – can it?'

'Most times when he's driving that stagecoach,' Caton said, 'Ed has a man sitting alongside him riding shotgun. That particular day, the senator had two armed lawmen riding herd on him, so Ed was up there on his own.' He paused, choosing his words. 'I know for sure Stan Coleman keeps something under his seat. Keeps it within easy reach. If he reaches for it as often as folks suggest—'

'Well I'll be damned,' McCrae cut in softly, and Caton smiled.

'You've heard that story?'

'Heard, but clean forgotten. Lax of me. Unprofessional.'

'A jug of rotgut, moonshine whiskey,' Caton mused. 'Ed's partial. Marshal Cole Banning's new in Dodge, been here six months so he doesn't know Ed all that well. If he did, and was wise to that driver's drinking habits. . . ?'

'Hold the presses,' McCrae said, and his chair went flying as he hurtled out through the door and clattered down the stairs.

ELEVEN

'Where's Gallant?'

Melody Lake was waiting for him when Stick McCrae rode down Front Street in some haste. They were together alongside the steel rails that split the street in two, in the saddle and holding their mounts on loose reins as the horses backed and nudged, tails flicking, heads tossing impatiently.

'Said he'd be here,' McCrae said, breathless. 'He's not, so that's too bad because he'll miss all the good stuff.'

'You got something from Caton?'

'Something extra special,' McCrae said. 'All you need to know is that Coleman is a drinker,' but he was shouting over his shoulder as he turned his horse and pulled away. Lake shook her head in frustration as she spurred to catch the racing newspaperman.

Stan Coleman lived in a small iron-roofed timber cottage on the outskirts of Dodge. McCrae and Lake dismounted and tied their horses to the picket fence. A woman was watching them from the patch of grass fronting the house.

Bosoms would describe her, McCrae thought; the word bosoms had surely been made with her in mind. She wore old serge pants and over them a loose blue smock. Her outstanding – McCrae smothered a grin – her outstanding bosoms had that smock shimmering down her front the way water cascades from a high rocky ledge. She was looking at McCrae with her lip curled. Her grey hair was snatched back in a bun. In her lined hand she held some kind of garden tool that looked dangerous.

'You after Stan?'

'We need to talk to him,' Melody said politely.

'You and most of Dodge,' the woman said. 'I'm Matilda, Stan's wife. He's on the back stoop doing some . . . well. . . .'

She led the way round the house, through ragged grass and some litter. The back gallery had a rotting rattan shade over its length and width. Stan Coleman was sitting in a battered armchair. He was small, all bone and sinewy, with a face like dried leather. Despite being out of the sun he wore a sweat-stained hat. Strands of grey hair straggled. His eyes were rheumy, but watchful. His right hand was dangling over the chair's padded arm. Close to his nicotine-stained fingers there was a round brown jug. His touch on the cool pottery was loving, a caress.

He saw Melody, and raised a hand to his hat brim.

'Know you,' he said in liquor-seasoned tones. 'Seen you sashaying about town. If I was twenty years younger. . . .'

'Fifty,' Matilda said. 'You'd need to be fifty years younger, and even then you wouldn't stand a chance, you old fool.'

'Stood a chance with you.'

'That's because I was a *young* fool.'

'Stayed foolish, but grew old,' Coleman said, and his laugh was a cackle.

The insults flew back and forth, but to Melody Lake it seemed like a performance, old phrases oft repeated, and the fondness they felt for each other was palpable in the hot air enclosed under the sagging rattan.

'I hate to interrupt a bruising contest,' she said, 'but can we call a truce and talk about the day Senator Slade was murdered.'

'By that Gallant feller,' Stan Coleman said.

'You sure about that?' said McCrae.

'Saw him. Recognized him. Hair like straw too long in the sun. Eyes? Hell, his eyes were holes in his face, could see straight through 'em to the clear blue skies.'

'Poetic,' Melody said. 'We could do with you on our newspaper. A way with words, and you're remarkably good at remembering details despite—'

'His fondness for good liquor?' Matilda had seen Melody's gaze linger pointedly on the brown jug, and leaped to her man's defence. 'Hellfire, Stan's been drinking since he was ten years old, after sixty years that moonshine whiskey's like pure creek water.'

'Every day,' Coleman said. 'Up there on that box, juggling three pairs of reins, sun a ball of fire and the hot dry wind in my face. A man could die,' he said plaintively, 'without something to wet his whistle.'

'So there can be no doubt,' Melody pressed. 'You'd been knocking back quantities of pure creek water, but you recognized the killer. It was the man you know as Born Gallant, and you'd swear to that under oath?'

'Well, no, just hold on right there,' Matilda Coleman said cautiously. She'd dropped into a chair, and was dabbing her glistening cheeks with a hand-kerchief. 'Saying Gallant's the man he knows is maybe Stan putting it a bit strong. When he says he recognized him, this English feller, he's using what you newspaper people might call poetic licence. Because, while he's never seen the man—'

'Have done! Seen him often.' Coleman snapped the contradiction.

'When's that, Stan? Gallant's always news. When he's in town, everybody talks, and I don't recall anyone seeing him in Dodge these past six months. Besides, you drive that big Concord to hell and gone seven days a week. You don't see me more than once in one of them blue moons, so how could you see an Englishman who's mostly somewhere else?'

'Recognized him,' Coleman said stubbornly. He lifted the big jug, took a deep swig, stared his defiance through watering eyes.

'Gallant was hot news six months ago, when he took off with that Flint boy,' Matilda said. 'When Ed did make it back to town, he'd prop up a bar in one of the saloons. Talk would always turn to Gallant. Everything about him. What he'd done, his looks, his crazy way of talking. So when Ed says he recognized the man. . . .'

'Hearsay,' Melody Lake said.

'Hear what?' asked Matilda, dabbing.

'It means that from what he'd heard in those saloons he visits, Ed thought he recognized Gallant,' Melody said. 'It's called hearsay and, in a court of law, hearsay carries no weight.'

'I've got the knife,' Stan Coleman blurted.

McCrae stared. 'I heard it was an ordinary Bowie knife killed Slade.'

'You think Jim Bowie's still out there makin' them?'

'No. Bowie's long gone. But how did you get hold of it?'

'Nobody riding shotgun with me, but the scatter-gun was there under the box alongside that jug. Gallant stuck that knife in the senator, thrust in clear to the hilt, and I was up on my pins with that scatter-gun and I let loose with both barrels and that Gallant feller' – he grimaced at McCrae's glare – 'he dropped the knife and he ran for his horse and was gone.'

'Why bring all this up?' Melody said. 'About the knife.'

'I told you, Bowie don't make 'em any more. Maybe never did, maybe only crafted the one made him famous. But there's a feller in Dodge does a mighty fine job, makes 'em special. Sure as the good Lord made green apples, this one was made for Gallant.'

'His name?'

'Ted.'

Melody smiled. 'We need more than that.'

'Hell, everyone in Dodge knows him as Ted.'

'Theodore,' Matilda said; she crushed her handkerchief into a ball. 'You'll find him on the south side of the railroad tracks. Theodore Bullock is Dodge City's blacksmith.'

Melody flashed McCrae a look. 'Isn't that where. . . ?

McCrae nodded. 'One more question before we go, ma'am,' he said. 'It's about Liam Dolan.'

'Dolan's dead.'

'Did he leave any kin?'

'A brother. Sean Dolan.'

Again Melody and McCrae exchanged glances.

'I said hearsay carries no weight,' Melody said, 'but it does have its uses. What does this Sean Dolan look like?'

'Rides a good horse,' Stan Coleman said. 'Thoroughbred, last I saw.'

'Wears his hair long, down to here,' Matilda said, and her fingers stroked to indicate. 'Going grey, but he likes that. Got eyes like . . . like sapphire gemstones gone all faded, washed out.'

She paused, and now the look she gave Melody Lake was filled with dread.

'My advice is to stay well clear of him. That man's as cruel as an Apache. Leave even a faint shadow crossing his path, and as a pretty little lawyer you can write out your own will document – because you're as good as dead.'

TWELVE

Gallant was grinning, wide blue eyes innocent.

'Absolutely correct, old boy, it really was a mistake having Theodore remove that iron from my ankles. Made a stunning weapon, if you'll pardon the pun, and if I'd known you were coming I wouldn't have baked a cake but—'

'Cut the silly talk, and get rid of that six-gun.'

'Your wish is my command,' Gallant said, 'or some such rot. Can't have an escaped prisoner running about the place armed and dangerous, frightening the horses. . . .'

He was moving while talking, his fingers touching the butt of the gun. His eyes were on the floor, as if looking for a clear place amidst all the metal junk, worn horseshoes, dropped tools and charcoal ash where he could drop the weapon. But his seemingly casual steps and willingness to comply with Madison's order had not only given Bullock a clear view of the deputy, they had drawn the deputy's eyes away from the blacksmith. He was watching Gallant – and that was a mistake.

Gallant's fingers lifted Flint's engraved six-gun out of its holster. He grinned again, held the shiny weapon aloft to reflect the forge's fiery glow, a hypnotist drawing the attention of his subject's eyes. As Madison instinctively, suspiciously, followed Gallant's every move, Bullock – a big man with a big man's deceptive speed – exploded into action.

His powerful legs drove him up off the three-legged stool. He twisted as he rose, reached backwards and down to grab one of the legs with his left hand. Still twisting, he straightened and used the impetus of his fast body-turn to throw the stool. It whirled under the chimney's cone and across the glowing charcoal. Madison, still watching Gallant, out of the corner of his eye saw it hurtling towards him. He lifted an arm to shield his head, but the stool was spinning. The three legs made the heavy wooden object confusing to follow, more dangerous. The edge of the seat cracked against Madison's forearm. That spun the stool. One of the legs came over. The hard end rammed into the hollow under his cheekbone. It was like being hit by a bullet. A tooth was broken off at the gum. He roared in pain, reeled backwards, clutching his face and spitting blood. His grip on the six-gun loosened. It fell from his grasp, clanged against the iron forge.

Bullock was already following the stool, acting on his advantage. Going round the forge after Madison would have wasted precious seconds. Instead, his hand again dipped and when it came up from the floor he was holding an iron shovel. His other arm came over.

Both big fists clamped close to the end of the long wooden handle. Snarling ferociously through his black beard, the blacksmith brought the shovel around in a wide sweeping move. The metal blade dipped as it crossed the forge. It scooped up a heap of the glowing charcoal. With a final flick of the wrists, Bullock flung the red-hot shower straight at Madison. It hissed as it flew, its passage through the air turning the red glow to white heat. This time the deputy's yell signified both agony and fear as he began flapping with both hands at his already smoking shirt and vest.

Born Gallant heard the terrible scream. He'd grimaced at the ferocity of Bullock's attack, but he had holstered the six-gun and was moving towards the door as the blacksmith sprang into action. Quickly though he moved, his thoughts were racing ahead of him. What of the other deputy, Deacon? On the buckboard he'd taken a hard blow from one of the iron fetters when Gallant had aimed a kick at his head, but he was a big, strong man. If he had recovered quickly he could be outside, waiting. On the other hand, if Deacon was still suffering and out of the fight, Madison could have enlisted other help. He and Deacon would be desperate to recapture Gallant and salvage their tattered reputations.

All this passed through Gallant's mind as he ran for the door. He could see his horse, still there, still waiting. Nostrils flared, eyes rolling, ears flattened, it was trembling with fear and surely about to turn tail and bolt. Gritting his teeth, silently begging the animal to wait just a little longer, Gallant reached the doorway. On the way out he snatched up the long-handled bolt cutters which Bullock had left leaning against the wall. Then he stepped swiftly from the gloom and intense, overpowering heat of the smithy, into more heat and bright and dazzling sunlight.

Ignoring the howls of pain behind him, half-shielded by the doorway, he spent precious seconds surveying the situation. Swift glances to left and right along the alleyway told him all he needed to know. To his left, perhaps thirty yards away, Deputy Deacon, his head swathed in a white bandage, was sitting slumped wearily astride his mount with a rifle held across his legs. No escape that way, Gallant thought wryly, without causing the man even more pain. To Gallant's right two mounted men blocked the only other way out of the alley. Once again there was a song in Born Gallant's heart. Hot blood coursed through his veins. The scent of battle was in the air, and he sniffed at it like a hunting cougar detecting the scent of prey.

Damn it, he thought, flinging himself at his mount and springing nimbly into the saddle, let poor old Deacon alone. The man was probably too concussed to see straight anyway, so attacking him in his weakened state would hardly be cricket. Two healthy armed men, however, were fair game, and Gallant had never been deterred by odds of a mere two to one.

Go for the jugular he thought, grinning savagely. With one hand he snapped the reins taut, pulled his horse's head around. With a whispered apology to the animal, he used his spurs with unusual cruelty. The horse squealed an injured protest, but leaped forward.

97

Like Deacon in the other direction, the two men at the end of the alley were about thirty yards away from the smithy. Gallant charged straight at them, taking the horse up to a full gallop. The sheer audacity of his action gave the men pause. Perhaps they had already been discomfited, puzzled, by the terrible sounds of human suffering emerging from Bullock's workshop.

Whatever the reason, Gallant had covered fifteen of the thirty yards before they reacted. Then they went for their guns. But a galloping horse can race over ground at forty miles an hour. Gallant, upright in the saddle, reins held tight in his left hand, was on the two men before their hands had touched a six-gun's butt. In his right hand he held the long-handled iron bolt cutters, swinging them vertically the way a polo player swings his full-length wooden mallet.

Gallant timed it so that the heavy iron jaws of the bolt cutters were on the upswing when he reached the two men. He drove his horse between them. The man on his right had been the first to react. His six-gun was half out of its holster. The swinging head of the bolt cutters drove upwards under the holster, carried on through to break the man's fingers and rip the six-gun from his hand, then it continued onwards and upwards into his armpit with enough power left to drive him sideways out of the saddle.

From behind Gallant there came the crack of a rifle. Deacon was retaining enough of his senses to pull a trigger. Still grinning, Gallant heard the swish of the bullet cutting the air above his head, heard a six-gun fire close by as the second man joined the action.

But that man was too late, and firing wildly. On and through Gallant rode, now flattened along his mount's neck with its mane in his face. He swung hard to the right and tore out of the alley.

THIRTEEN

'Very little,' Born Gallant said. 'Apart from having both ankles free of those confounded iron fetters, I got nothing much of importance from Theodore Bullock.'

'Ted,' Melody Lake said.

'Thought Ted was short for Edward?'

'Probably is. But according to Stan Coleman Theodore Bullock's known to one and all as Ted.'

'Interesting, but if that's the best Coleman had to offer we've all wasted hours we really cannot spare.'

'Who said that was all?' Melody said.

Gallant, Stick McCrae and Melody Lake were sitting on warm grass in the shade of cottonwood trees to the east of Dodge City. Melody was cross-legged, fanning herself with a leafy twig. McCrae was sitting with his back to a tree, Gallant lying full-length on a mossy slope with his hands behind his head. Insects hummed lazily. Water tinkled over rocks in a nearby creek.

All of which, Gallant thought hazily, was a welcome,

pleasant change.

Flattened along his speeding mount's neck, he had burst from the end of the alley with little thought other than to get clear of Deacon, Madison and their two hired hands; although, after his polo-inspired work with the long bolt-cutters he was pretty sure that help would now be down to just the one man.

With freedom constantly on his mind he had slowed his horse's insane gallop and done some fast thinking. Not much of that was needed: it had been clear to him ever since his first escape that riding boldly through the town was out of the question.

Easing his mount across the railroad tracks and away from the midday hustle and bustle, he had cantered towards the town's southern outskirts. A few minutes later, he had encountered McCrae and Lake riding in the opposite direction. Finished with the Colemans, they had decided that if they were going to discover what had delayed Gallant, the blacksmith's smithy was the obvious place to start.

Meeting Gallant had made that unnecessary. Together again, they had put the town behind them and ridden in a leisurely fashion eastwards, with their eyes skinned for a suitably pleasant place to rest, eat and share information.

Melody Lake had biscuits in her saddlebags. They all carried water. She was crunching one of the biscuits now, and Gallant, from his horizontal position, was studying her smug expression with great interest.

'All right,' he said at last, 'I'll bite. What else did you get from our lying – no, let's say our well-intentioned but *misguided* stagecoach driver?'

'This,' Stick McCrae said. Reaching behind him, he plucked a large Bowie knife from his leather belt then held it aloft. The broad steel blade caught the sunlight filtering through the trees. It made a fearsome sight.

'Well I'll be double damned,' Gallant said softly, lifting his head. 'Is that the ghastly weapon that did the deed?'

'Certainly is,' McCrae said.

'Shouldn't it be evidence? Held for safe keeping by Banning?'

'Apparently Coleman was happy to tell his tale, but kept possession of the knife to himself.'

'And he gave it to you?'

'I think he realized the risk he was taking now that a man who writes for newspapers knew what he'd done.'

'Let me have it, Stick.'

'I could take that request the wrong way, but I'll assume you mean you want the knife.'

'I've got an idea,' Gallant said, 'that at some time not too far ahead I'll find a use for it.'

'And that,' Melody Lake said, 'has got me seriously worried. But, more to the point,' she went on, rolling her eyes charmingly at the unintentional pun, 'that knife, which did the deed, was probably forged by your new friend Ted.'

'I'm impressed at his skill,' Gallant said, 'but that gets us . . . where, exactly?'

'Ted's a town blacksmith fashioning horseshoes daily and in their hundreds, but these exquisitely crafted knives he makes only rarely. He'll keep records. Know those special clients clutching handfuls of dollar bills who came to him with an avaricious gleam in their eyes. It's highly likely that, without realizing it, Ted Bullock knows the name of the man who murdered Senator Slade.'

'Glory be!' Gallant sat up, suddenly alert. 'That being the case, it looks like a hasty return to that shabby smithy—'

'Hold your horses,' McCrae cut in. 'That's only part of what we got from the Colemans. On the way out I asked another question, and this one bore ripe fruit. It seems the late and extremely unlamented Liam Dolan has a brother.'

'And we got a description,' Melody said.

'Ah.' Gallant nodded, the humour fading from his blue eyes. 'Let me guess. Tall lean feller, shoulder-length hair goin' grey, face carved from stone and eyes like snow-melt waters.'

'All of that, yes, and he rides thoroughbred horses,' Melody said.

'And lives where?'

'Got that as we walked out,' McCrae answered. 'Sean Dolan is a wealthy rancher. His land lies close to Wichita. From what Matilda Coleman told us I'd say he and Guthrie Flint are neighbours.'

'But not friends?'

McCrae shrugged. 'No idea. I'd have said not, but Flint has now proved that, like Dolan, he can stomach extreme violence if it becomes necessary. Another thing Matilda said was that Dolan is a cold-blooded killer, so while not exactly enjoying his brutality, it's possible you got off lightly.'

'All of which leaves me with a dilemma,' Gallant said. 'There's Sean Dolan, the man who hung me from a tree and had me flogged. That's something I'd like to ... let's say I'd like to discuss it with him. Looked at dispassionately, though, it's obviously of lesser importance than the information Ted Bullock might be able to provide.'

'Maybe not,' McCrae said. 'Didn't we start thinking along the lines that your flogging by Dolan could mean he's linked to the killing of Slade?'

'We did, but I've decided it's unlikely. What is certain is that if Bullock comes up with a name that leads Cole Banning to Senator Slade's killer, it would take away that damn rope I can feel tightening around my neck.'

'So you end up weighing what has happened against what might happen,' Melody said, and there was compassion in her voice. 'The flogging is in the past, Born, and cannot be changed. The gallows is shadowing your future. My advice, as a lawyer, would be to go back into town and from Theodore Bullock get the name of the man who asked him to fashion a knife. But the choice has to be yours – so what's it to be?'

FOURTEEN

They rode east across Kansas in the late afternoon, Gallant and McCrae, figuring that they would get to the Dolan spread round about nightfall. If they then waited the short time until full darkness, they would have a good chance of approaching the house unseen.

Melody Lake rode west, into Dodge City.

While the dark-haired young woman had sat cross-legged on the lush grass and told Gallant that the choice of where to go next had to be his, Gallant had been watching her closely but hearing the echoes of words spoken by Theodore Bullock. The blacksmith had called Melody feisty, and she was certainly that. But the big man had also said that the courageous young woman should be kept well clear when the rough stuff started. That advice had opened Gallant's eyes, forced him to realize that he had for too long been allowing, even encouraging, Melody to risk her life on his behalf. That made his decision an easy one.

Sean Dolan was a cold-blooded killer. When ordering Gallant's flogging, he had been accompanied by tough, unshaven characters with eyes as mean as Dolan's were pale and an easy familiarity with handguns and rifles. Outlaws, mavericks, whatever one liked to call them, they were men certain to react with extreme violence if crossed. Those men worked for Dolan. They, and others of their kind, would be at his ranch. Approaching the house in darkness on foot without being detected was possible, but could not be guaranteed. If the attempt failed, it would draw the ire of the ranch's owner, and almost certainly a hail of hot lead. Dolan's defence policy on his home spread would be to shoot first, ask questions later if anyone was left standing.

The Dolan spread would be no place for a young woman.

The alternative was much less fraught. Melody worked for Tom Caton at the *Dodge City Times*. She was a familiar figure often seen about town. Riding into Dodge posed no risk for her. At his blacksmith's workshop Bullock would greet her courteously, listen to her questions, look through his records. Melody was at ease with the printed word. She could, if necessary, help the blacksmith with his search for the name that would save Born Gallant from the gallows.

Yet even knowing that Melody Lake would be safe gave Born Gallant no comfort, for he was riding into the unknown with Stick McCrae. Getting close to Sean Dolan would put McCrae in great danger, and Gallant was becoming increasingly uneasy about the way both

McCrae and Lake were involved in troubles that were his, and his alone.

He had first met Lake and McCrae in Kansas City when tracking down crooked members of the Consolidated Cattle Growers' Association. That had also led to wrongdoings at the Pinkerton Detective Agency, and a later violent confrontation with the massive half-breed Sundown Tancred at Salvation Creek. Months later, McCrae and Lake had unexpectedly appeared on the scene in Dodge City in the aftermath of Gallant's snatching young Billie Flint from the gallows; once again they had entered enthusiastically into a hunt for killers that saw them putting their lives in danger.

It couldn't go on.

Born Gallant had crossed the Atlantic because, after a life spent seeking adventure, excitement and thrills across several continents, often in the uniform of the British Army, he could not face years as an English aristocrat attending endless soirées and donning a red coat to ride a horse across muddy fields chasing a terrified fox. Still too young to settle down, he had given his blessing and his title to his sister (still wasn't sure if that was legal) and sailed to the New World. There, comforted by the thought of unlimited funds there for him to draw from a New York bank, he had once again become a knight errant. Or should that be, he thought with a wry grin, a silly ass turned drifting hobo who always got into scrapes and had so far escaped by the skin of his teeth?

Just as Gallant had been when he set out to paint

the world red, McCrae and Lake were young. Like Gallant, they were hungry for adventure, excitement, thrills, and saw no risk in facing terrible danger, for it was their belief that injury or death happened to other people. But their lives lay ahead of them. Sooner or later the excitement of what they were doing would fade. They would wince at the memory of cuts and bruises and broken limbs, be shocked at feeling the first tremors of fear when staring into the muzzle of a cocked six-gun, then look at hard Born Gallant: foot-loose, feckless and rich, and begin to ask themselves what the hell they were playing at.

That moment couldn't come too soon for Gallant. When his two loyal companions rode off into the sunset to get on with their lives, they would take with them his new and totally unexpected feelings of guilt.

But, for now, there was Sean Dolan.

FIFTEEN

'The man who drew the plans for the buildings making up this ranch,' Born Gallant said, 'did it on a morning when he had a raging hangover and tumbled out of bed on the wrong side.'

'No.' McCrae shook his head. 'We can assume it was Dolan. What he did was stay up all one night staring out at the darkness. In between taking money off cattlemen to let those herds through, he had to cope with Indians who were going on the warpath. He'd have been pondering on how best he could make himself secure. We're looking at the result.'

'Stayed up all night where?'

'I'd say the old ranch house is down there in the dip, with the barns, the bunkhouse, the corrals.' McCrae waved a hand at a cluster of buildings. Night mist was curling across the yard, turned into veils of white smoke by the moonlight. The timber structures appeared to be floating. Some of those buildings were in darkness; in the windows of others, oil lamps glowed.

'So when dawn was breaking, the rising sun lit up the brow of that hill,' Gallant said, 'Dolan decided to build himself a fortress. Or, at the very least, a house so positioned that it would be impossible for intruders to approach undetected.'

They had bidden farewell to Melody Lake, and left the outskirts of Dodge City in the late afternoon as planned. But the scant information McCrae had got from Matilda Coleman about the location of the Dolan spread saw them riding some distance down several wrong trails before eventually coming across the rocky bluff she had described as a landmark. They had ridden for another hour, the last half in darkness. When their horses swished through grass wet with dew and they saw before them what had to be Sean Dolan's place, a bright moon was floating behind hazy clouds.

'It's an ordinary house with the usual windows and doors,' Gallant said, 'but around it there's no trees, no scrub, and the land falls away on all sides. If I was an army general and that was the enemy entrenched up there, I'd reckon the only way to beat them would be to lay siege and starve 'em out.'

'Is that a plan?'

'It's a cry for help, an invitation for you to suggest an alternative.'

They had moved through the last stand of trees before coming to the slope leading down to the Dolan spread. In a landscape turned eerily flat by the full moon, they sat for some minutes in silence, their horses on the fringe of the trees. McCrae was smoking a cigarette, the glowing tip cupped in his hand.

Gallant was simply looking and listening, working on the principle that ignoring a problem would see the solution rise out of the subconscious. Faintly on the night air he could hear the wail of a harmonica. Someone was singing in a voice made raucous by too many cigarettes and too much drink. He was way out of tune. From what Gallant was hearing he surmised that the lights they could see were glowing in the bunkhouse.

'He's a rancher, Stick,' he said at last, 'and you could be right about him being guided by the dawn's early light. But I reckon he built the house up there because his wife wanted to be well away from those rough, rowdy cowpokes, in a house with a very special view. And I'll tell you something else. When those lights are extinguished in the bunkhouse, there'll be nobody awake within ten miles of this place. Also, no scrub and no trees makes for easy, silent riding, and I never did like walking uphill.'

'Two curving tracks up to the house,' McCrea mused. 'The one leading off the trail we came in on joins that wider one coming up from the ranch yard.' He looked at Gallant. 'Obvious one to use is the one off the trail.'

'Better still if we use neither, wouldn't you say? That house on the hill lies east to west. Fenced all round, big wide gallery out front where I think I can see a table and chairs, reinforce my idea of Dolan's other half wanting a home with a view.'

'If we'd arrived earlier she'd have been out there sipping cocktails,' McCrae said.

111

'Watching the fiery ball of the setting sun sinking in the south-west,' Gallant contributed. He smiled. 'But all that's fantasy, and time-wasting, and the point I'm making is that on the west side of the house there's no windows. A sensible man wanting to get close to Dolan without being seen wouldn't go trotting his horse up those tracks. He'd go a half mile back up the trail, then cut across the grass and up the slope to that blank side of the house.'

'Getting close,' McCrae said, 'is not my idea of sensible.'

'That's what I'm here for, but you don't need to be part of it. You've come this far, and I'm grateful. But this is my fight, and it could get nasty. I don't want your death on my conscience.'

'Didn't realize it was a fight. Recall you saying you intended discussing with him that business of hanging and whipping. But that's by the by. This is the first time I've heard you show that kind of concern for my welfare. You been doing some thinking?'

'Too much, probably too serious, and we're both talking like old women,' Gallant said. He was watching the last light winking out in the bunkhouse, imagining the harmonica player taking the instrument from his lips and blowing it clear of spit, listening to the silence settle over the Dolan spread.

'Having given due consideration to what I said, are you in or out?'

'In for a penny, in for a pound,' Stick McCrae said, and touched boot-heels to his horse. 'Come on, Gallant, what the hell are you waiting for?'

*

There was the scent of wood-smoke in the air. They'd got close to the house in the manner Gallant had suggested, riding in on the blind side. Well, at least up as close as the fence. But there they'd paused. They had to get round the house, and in through one of the doors. But which one, and how was it to be done?

'Back or front?' McCrae asked, guessing his thoughts.

'Good question. Can you hear anything?'

'Thought I heard movement inside.'

'Ears like a bat. There's a wind getting up, could be a loose shutter banging. But if you're right and it was in the house, smashing down doors could be counterproductive.'

'Meaning we'd end up dead?'

'It would make our creeping up like thieves in the night utterly pointless.' Gallant hesitated. 'Damn it, we sneaked up because being seen could have drawn gunfire. Now we're here, let's act like gents. We'll tie the horses, walk up and knock politely on the front door.'

'With guns drawn.'

'Pouched, but each of us carrying a rifle. Make sure there's a shell in the breech.'

'Long guns'll be an encumbrance.'

'If he lets us in.'

'Will he have a choice?'

Gallant grinned. 'Not once he's opened the door. Come on, it's time for action.'

113

They tied the horses, slid rifles out of saddle boots. The fence was a simple high affair of sturdy posts and horizontal rails with wide gaps between them. Stepping through was easier than climbing over. With Gallant in the lead they padded across the grass and round the blind side of the house. That brought them to the gallery that stretched all the way across the front of the building. It was raised from the ground on wooden stumps and had fancy rails. Again, it was easier to step through the wide spacing. The boards under foot creaked as they made for the front door, but Gallant knew the sharp noise was of no importance. They were going to walk up to the house and knock on the door. A totally silent approach would raise suspicions, put Dolan on his guard.

'Ready?' Gallant said softly over his shoulder, and he caught McCrae's nod.

The door was heavy oak, with iron fittings. A rap with knuckles was unlikely to be heard. Gallant lifted his Winchester high and pounded on the door several times with the butt. The noise was like the rolling of thunder overhead.

'Jesus Christ!' McCrae said.

Gallant held up a warning hand. Inside the house a man had cursed loudly. Boots clumped, drawing closer. Then the door was wrenched open and pulled wide.

Sean Dolan was in his undershirt, his pants tucked into tooled leather boots. His long hair was damp, there was fury in his pale eyes.

'I'm telling you, for the last time, you will not

disturb me after. . . .'

Then he stopped, saw who had come calling and said, 'What the *hell*—'

Born Gallant took a short step and, using the same force that he'd employed when pounding the door, he hit Dolan full in the face with the butt of his rifle.

SIXTEEN

Staggering backwards, eyes glazed and empty of any sense after the fierce blow from the rifle butt, the rancher's legs crumpled and he went down as if poleaxed. Gallant and McCrae stepped over the threshold and grabbed hold of a leg apiece. They dragged him into the room. Dolan was dazed but not unconscious, snuffling wetly. Pulled face down, limp arms trailing, he left a long smear of bright-red blood across the polished boards.

They flung him on to what looked like the pelt of a full-grown cougar, one of several animal skins covering most of the floor between what Gallant could see was expensive furniture: stuffed easy chairs, oak cabinets with crystal decanters and glasses, a refectory table with one end close to the window; on its glossy surface stood three silver candelabra bearing unlit pink candles with blackened wicks.

McCrae bent, seized hold of an arm and turned Dolan over, taking his face out of the thick animal fur so that he could breathe. Still holding the rifle with blood on its butt, Gallant went back and quietly shut the door.

The light from the high moon flooded in through the window. It touched the end of the coffee table, pooled across it, highlighting the glossy surface, then weakened. From there on in the room was in darkness apart from that faint and fading reflected light; Gallant and McCrae had expected that from their observation of the house from the high ground and from their reflections in the darkened windows as they'd crossed the gallery. Elsewhere, lamplight seeped in from a second room seen through an open door at the rear of the living-room.

'What's through there?'

Dolan dragged a hand over his bloody face. He turned, spat a fragment of tooth, shook his head.

Gallant stepped in, drew back his foot and delivered a powerful kick to the body. The rancher's mouth gaped wide. Gallant thought he heard the crack of one or more ribs breaking.

'I asked a question.'

A deep, shuddering breath. Eyes widening in shock, a quickly suppressed moan, the realization that the simple act of breathing causes agony when the ribcage is damaged.

'Kitchen. That's where I was—'

'Where's your wife?'

The colourless eyes narrowed, filled with hatred. But there was a slow and visible relaxation of tensed muscles. An intelligent man was coming to terms with his injuries, with his predicament. With that realization came acceptance, followed by the beginning of a cool and measured calculation of chances and their risks: even in his distressed state the man's menace was palpable.

'Is she upstairs?' Gallant said, watching the thinking man with a wry smile that betokened supreme confidence. 'In bed, is she, waiting for you?'

A nod.

'Anyone else in the house?'

'No. My son lives away from here. If he had been here with me it would be you lying on the floor hurt bad.'

The voice began weak, strengthened with each word. At the end of the little speech Dolan twisted on the floor, got his legs under him and stood up. He was a big man. He stood awkwardly, lopsided, because of the damaged ribs. The blood dribbling on to his white undershirt from his broken mouth seemed not to bother him. He looked down at the cougar's pelt, at the blood now matting the fur; he grimaced and stepped on to polished boards.

Stick McCrae reached back to place his rifle on the table, then drew his six-gun.

'No need for that.' Dolan indicated his hips, the lack of a gunbelt or weapon, and hawked noisily to clear the blood clogging his throat. 'Unarmed, as you can see – and I know why you're here.' He looked at Gallant.

'You sure about that?'

'Retribution. Isn't that so? Payback for what was inflicted on you. An eye for an eye.'

'That was your motive when you hung me from a tree and had me flogged. An eye for an eye. You were exacting payment for what happened to your brother. But your brother killed a young boy—'

'A stray bullet—'

'—and was a crooked lawman to boot. He framed young Billie Flint, tried to hang him. When that didn't work, he or one of his men shot him in the back.'

'And you are . . . what? Judge, jury, executioner?' Dolan snorted, limped across to a low oak chiffonier. He leaned an elbow on the dark wood for support, rattled a decanter against a crystal glass as he poured whiskey and knocked it back in one swallow. When Dolan looked at the glass he saw that his blood was staining its rim. He turned, leaned back, glared his fury at Gallant.

'Don't know why I asked. You haven't the brains or the guts to be any one of those, Gallant.' Now the rancher was openly mocking. 'What you are is a pathetically soft, puffed-up English aristocrat strutting pompously across a hard land – and you're way out of your depth.'

'Let's say you're right. And let's say that Senator Slade, politician with soft white hands that had never done a day's work, was the American version of that pathetic Englishman. If he was, that made us soul mates. When I asked if you were sure you knew why I was here tonight, you said it was for retribution. You hit the nail on the head, Dolan, but you had the wrong person in mind.'

Gallant was thinking on his feet, concocting a story

that would fit the occasion. Dolan was frowning as he digested Gallant's words.

'What's that you're saying? That you were after retribution . . . for the *senator*? For Slade? What the hell are you talking about? I had nothing to do with his death.'

'My flogging was nothing. I've endured tougher trials and tribulations when strutting pompously – as you eloquently put it – across the arid Indian sub-continent that makes the American West look like powder-puff land. So that rifle-butt in your face was satisfaction enough for me. But Slade cannot get satisfaction, because he's dead – and I think you hired a man who looked uncannily like me to drive a Bowie knife through his heart.'

'Why would I do that? Slade was a good friend of Guthrie Flint, a fellow politician. Slade lost his young son to a stray bullet. Flint. . . .' Dolan turned to pour another shot of whiskey, knocked it back, hissed through his teeth as the raw alcohol seared his bloody gums. 'Flint,' he went on, again clearing his throat, 'Flint's son Billie died—'

'Was murdered by your brother.'

'— in those woods to the south of Dodge. What you thought of my brother Liam is neither here nor there. I'm a prosperous rancher, well respected. I'd met Slade. He'd called here for drinks when visiting Flint, who lives close by – no more than five miles away. I felt sympathy for Slade's loss, and sympathy for Flint. He may be on his way to Washington, but he's now lost two wives and one of his sons.'

'One of? Billie was an only child.'

'To Flint's first wife. His second wife brought a boy with her when she moved in.'

'Making him Flint's stepson,' Gallant said. 'But he doesn't live with Flint?'

'Never did.'

'Did he take Flint's name?'

'Nope.'

And then Dolan exposed bloody teeth in a grin as, somewhere at the back of the house, a door slammed shut.

Gallant's eyes narrowed. He shot a glance at McCrae, jerked his head. McCrae, still holding his six-gun, went fast across the room. He hesitated at the door, listening, pistol held high. Then he went through into the kitchen.

'He's wasting his time,' Dolan said.

'So that was someone going out, not coming in?'

McCrae came back into the room. He was shaking his head.

'If your wife's gone to raise the alarm,' Gallant said, 'it's she who's wasting her time. I've done enough, heard enough. By the time she gets to the bunkhouse we'll be out of here, away and gone.'

'Oh, my Jen went out a while ago. She must have left the back door open in her haste. I guess the wind caught it.'

Lolling back against the chiffonier, Dolan was relaxed, watching with amusement as a variety of expressions raced across Gallant's face. McCrae cursed softly and turned to head for the front window.

From there he would be able to see down the long slope to the ranch yard, see any sign of movement, of men emerging from the bunkhouse.

Before he had reached the table they heard the back door crash open and bang against an unseen wall. At the same time the front door burst open. Pale moonlight flooded in, lighting the trail of blood smeared across the dark room's polished floor. Then the moonlight was blotted by shadows. A man charged in, closely followed by another. With the light at their backs they were dark and sinister shapes looming large and menacing. But they were men none the less, humans bearing shiny six-guns. Hurriedly answering the woman's call for help, they had tumbled out of their beds. They were bareheaded, their hair tousled, pants hastily thrown on and grey undershirts hanging over hard bellies.

But they had not forgotten their gunbelts. In too much of a hurry to buckle them around their waists, they had them looped over their shoulders. Their big fists, clutching six-guns, moved constantly from side to side, covering the room.

Gallant's immediate thought was: *End of the line. These two here and another coming in fast the back way leaves no way out, nowhere to hide.*

SEVENTEEN

What could be said about Stick McCrae?

Days later, weeks later, when Gallant recounted with suitable awe the journalist's heroic actions on that moonlit night on Sean Dolan's spread near the Kansas town of Wichita, he had no need to resort to embellishment. He simply told the unvarnished, unbelievable truth.

'What Stick did that night,' Gallant was often heard to say, 'also gave me the chance to prove Sean Dolan wrong. He'd called me a pathetic, soft, Englishman. He ended up eating those words.'

Gallant had no idea what McCrae's thoughts were when the two armed Dolan men burst in through the front door. Shock? Horror? Despair? Or perhaps numbness? Although, considering what followed, that last was surely out of the question. Before the two panting gunmen could steady themselves after their fast run up the moonlit slope from the ranch's yard, the newspaperman flung himself into action.

The long refectory table with its silver candelabra was positioned along the room's length, front to back, the near end some six feet away from the window. At each end there was a chair with a high open back and a basket-weave seat; the far one occupied the short space left for it between table and window.

McCrae pouched his six-gun and took a couple of fast steps. Without slowing he kicked the near chair out of his way and launched himself in a flat dive at the table. He landed on his belly, slid head first along the glossy surface. The Winchester rifle he had earlier placed there he snatched up in passing. Each silver candelabrum in turn was knocked aside, to fall with a clatter and bounce across the hard floor, the first was butted with the crown of his head, the second and third were swept away with his free arm. Then, the instant before he reached the end of the table, he twisted and pulled his bent legs round so that he could land feet first on the other chair.

As he did so there was a ripping sound: the basket-weave seat had given way, tearing beneath his weight. McCrae, finding himself falling sideways, recovered fast. He slammed a hand on the table to steady himself as his feet found purchase on the chair's frame. Now clutching his Winchester in both hands, he threw himself – a rolling, balled-up human cannon ball – through the big window. Glass shattered, shards flying high and glittering in the moonlight. The window's frame splintered. Most of the shattered timber was carried out by McCrae, draped around his shoulders.

The two gunmen reacted as Stick McCrae had anticipated. Their heads shot around to follow his move. Instinctively, they half-turned their bodies, swung their six-guns towards the flying newspaperman. But he was too fast. One of them got off a single shot. It scored a white gouge in the table's polished surface, hissed away and buried itself in the wall. The two men's eyes widened in disbelief as McCrae slid across the table, somersaulted, and left the room in a shower of broken glass.

Before they could recover from the shock, Gallant was moving.

He leaped at Dolan. The rancher was still lolling against the chiffonier, but his bloodied face looked stunned as he watched McCrae cutting lengthy gouges in the expensive table's top and sending precious silver candelabra clattering across the floor, demolishing a window. Again Gallant used his rifle, but this time with calculated force: taking a short swing as he moved in he whacked the side of the barrel against Dolan's temple. Hard enough to make him dazed, but light enough to leave him standing on wobbly pins.

Gallant grabbed him left-handed by his undershirt, swung him away from the chiffonier and stepped behind him. Swiftly shifting his grip he looped his left arm around the rancher's throat. Tightened it. Heard Dolan begin to choke. Then, six-gun in hand, the third gunman walked in from the kitchen. He was a raw-boned man, fully dressed in range clothes and with a look of quiet competence and authority. He took in the situation at a glance: the shattered window,

Dolan held in a stranglehold by Gallant, who was using the rancher as a human shield. Confident of his own prowess with a six-gun, the man swiftly calculated that he could shoot Gallant without endangering Dolan's life. He slapped his left hand over his right so that his six-gun was in a two-handed grip. He smirked as he brought it up, and Gallant found himself staring into the black hole of its muzzle, contemplating his last seconds on earth.

Still clamping his arm around Dolan's throat hard enough to stop him breathing, Gallant flipped his rifle up between the rancher's back and his own belly and, without taking aim, squeezed the trigger. A black hole to match his six-gun's muzzle appeared under the lean man's nose. The bullet's velocity knocked him off his feet. He went over backwards, hit the floor hard and lay still.

'And now,' Gallant called to the two other gunmen, 'we negotiate.' With a malign smile he tightened his hold on Dolan's throat.

The silence that settled over the room after the explosion of violence left ears buzzing, ringing. Dolan had for the moment given up his struggle, knowing it was useless to fight against Gallant's iron grip. His muscles lost some of their tenseness and, behind him, Gallant condescended to ease the pressure on his victim's throat and allow him to breathe.

Then the first two gunmen reacted. One went left, the other right. In that big room they outflanked Gallant. He was behind Dolan, could swing him either way; but swinging Dolan sideways to shield himself from one gunman on that side left him wide open on the other. Nevertheless he was forced to do just that as one of the gunmen blasted a shot that ricocheted off the chiffonier. Then the other gunman fired. The bullet plucked at Gallant's shirt. He felt the sweat break out on his forehead.

'You're done for,' Dolan croaked. He struggled jerkily, ineffectually, and was repaid for his efforts as Gallant resumed the pressure exerted by his arm, which now gripped like an iron band across Dolan's throat.

Then both gunmen moved in at the same time. Grinning, the leaner of the two stepped in close. Gallant recognized him as the man who had smoked a cigarette while watching his stocky companion carry out the flogging. Dolan suddenly went limp in his grip. His chin was forced back by the muscular forearm, but Gallant was forced to lean back to support the sudden dead weight. Hands reached for him, from one side, then from the other. Fingers clawed at his hair, took hold. . . .

The rifle shot was a blast that brought a shower of splinters down from directly above the struggling men. Then a voice roared a message meant solely for the rancher.

'Dolan, I have your wife.'

Gallant slapped at the hand clutching his hair, felt the fingers release their grip.

'She's outside on the gallery,' Stick McCrae went on, 'in a position of great discomfort.' His tall figure stood, a figure of menace, outlined in the doorway. Shards of broken glass were caught by the moonlight, sparkling in his hair. He was holding a rifle with smoke trickling from the muzzle.

'I used the lasso rope from my horse,' McCrae went on. 'Put a noose around her neck. Stood her on one of your fancy chairs. Tossed the rope over one of your gallery's high beams. When the end fell I pulled it tight and tied it to the gallery railings.'

Dolan was breathing hoarsely. His feet had again taken his weight. Gallant had slackened his strangle-hold, but not too much.

'I'm going to start counting,' McCrae said. 'With each count I'll take a step backwards. I estimate it'll take ten steps. You release Gallant now, Dolan – or on that tenth step I'll kick away the chair.'

EIGHTEEN

'Dolan really had no choice,' Gallant said. 'Stick using his wife as an aid to negotiation had effectively tied his hands, as it were.'

'So he let you both go.'

'With a heavy heart, a bloody face, and vile threats. It seems the man I plugged with my trusty rifle was his foreman. Luckily, the two men he employed to help him with my flogging were outsiders without any interest in the Dolan ranch. My killing of that foreman left them unmoved, and without any thought of revenge.'

Melody Lake shook her head. 'Nevertheless, it really was a skin of the teeth escape,' she said in disbelief. 'And what about you, Stick? I've known you as a mild man, wouldn't hurt a fly, yet you used that woman, threatened to hang her on Dolan's gallery.'

'There's no need to believe it,' McCrae said, 'because it was pure bluff. Dolan was having trouble breathing, so thinking straight was impossible. His wife had run down to the bunkhouse, and stayed there. There wasn't enough time between me going out through the window and appearing at his front door, to get his wife noosed up and on a chair.'

'You do understand that it won't be a whipping next time,' Melody said to Gallant. 'Dolan's always held you responsible for his brother's death all those months ago. Now, from what you've told me, you've done serious damage to his face with the butt of your rifle, and that same rifle's killed his straw boss. However – and this may surprise you – despite all that he holds you responsible for, friend Dolan is not the worst of your troubles.'

They were camped high up in the woods to the south of Dodge City. All too aware that he was still a hunted man, to avoid the town Gallant had chosen the route that curved to the south from Wichita then swung sharply north. His plan had been to spend the night there and let Stick McCrae head into Dodge the next morning to find and talk to Melody.

In a fine show of female intuition, Melody had guessed what he would do and, after leaving Theodore Bullock's smithy in the late afternoon, had herself ridden south. She'd walked her horse up through the woods. Always nervous at night in the darkness of a thick forest, she had been in an uneasy half-doze with her back against a tree when Gallant and Stick McCrae had appeared out of the gathering dusk.

'More bad news can wait,' Gallant said now. 'First, tell us what you got from Bullock.'

'We found the name. Frank Weston. It was quite a task. Most of Bullock's paperwork has curled or got gummed up with the heat of that place, and his pen-manship is awful.'

'And this Weston lives where?'

'Kansas, Bullock thinks. Couldn't narrow it down any further.'

'Which makes it about as much help,' Gallant said ruefully, 'as a spoonful of salt to a man dying of thirst in the desert.'

'And Kansas,' Melody Lake said, watching him, 'is about to get too hot for a certain English gentleman. Madison and Deacon slunk into Banning's office with their tails between their legs. He now knows you're on the loose.'

'If they told their story, why are you not suffering as I did in one of those awful cells? And why is Stick being hunted like a rabid dog?'

'Because I don't think those two deputies are willing to admit they suffered cuts and bruises giving up their captive to a couple of town softies.'

'So is Banning raising a posse?'

'I don't know. But as marshal he has to be seen doing something. The Slade killing is big news nation-wide.'

'But we're probably safe here until first light?'

'I'd say so.'

'So we make the most of that time,' McCrae said. 'Because while we learned two things today, only one is of help, and not much at that. We know that Dolan flogging Gallant has no connection to Slade's killing, so that's out of the way. But the name Melody got from Bullock is not going to clear Gallant unless we can find the man.'

*

131

They'd made their camp a little way inside the woods, still at the top of the hillside covered by trees. Their horses were tethered to trees on the wood's fringes, some fifty yards from the campsite. It there was trouble, and they could reach those horses, they had that clear escape route to open ground to the south.

They made a small fire, cooked a meal from supplies Melody had thoughtfully brought in her saddlebags, then sat around with the light of the flames flickering on their faces. The eerie effect on their countenances added to Melody's unease. She visibly jumped when, somewhere down the slope on the Dodge City side of the woods, a night animal crackled scrub as it stalked its prey.

Gallant, deep in thought, had been silent while eating and drinking the strong black coffee. Now, sitting on a log, he prodded the fire with a stick and sent a shower of sparks flying into the overhanging branches. He pinged the end of the stick against the hanging coffee pot.

'A name with no face,' he said. 'But if Weston is the man we want, we know what he looks like.'

'Looks like you,' Melody said. 'He must do, for the frame-up to work, but we need more than that.'

'OK,' Gallant said, 'so what else do we know?'

'The answers to two questions could help,' Stick McCrae said. 'The first of which is the obvious one: who benefits from Slade's death? The second is more of a puzzle: why frame Gallant for the killing?'

Melody sipped her coffee, her eyes dark in the firelight.

'Slade was senator for Kansas,' she said. 'He needs replacing.'

'Damn it, that's right,' Gallant said softly. 'If we follow that line of thinking, we've got the motive and something to work on. The man taking over Slade's office is going to be a prominent Kansas politician, and if we're on the right track he's going to be someone not afraid to get his hands dirty.'

'Guthrie Flint,' McCrae said.

In the sudden silence all that could be heard was the crackle and hiss of the fire. Then, downslope, not too far away, another animal – or the same one still blundering – crackled its way through the dry undergrowth.

'We now know to our cost what Flint is capable of,' Gallant said at last. 'But there's something else I've only just this minute recalled. You'll remember I spent time with the Pinkerton Detective Agency. Six months ago, when we visited Flint during the hunt for the killer of Slade's son, he said he'd caught sight of me one afternoon in Kansas City. I'd been deep in conversation with Bill Pinkerton. Flint said Bill was a good friend of his, and that he spoke highly of me – he told Flint I was a good detective, impossible to shake off once on the scent.'

'If Flint got where he is using dirty tricks – and some politicians believe that they can resign themselves to lifelong obscurity if they don't – there'll be skeletons rattling their bones in his cupboards,' Melody said.

'Forget the dirty tricks, concentrate on the Slade killing,' Gallant said, suppressed excitement in his voice. 'For Flint, killing Slade would clear the way to high office. But he could still hear Pinkerton's words about me. Framing me for the killing would get rid of a dangerous former Pinkerton operative.'

'So we go and put that to Flint,' Melody said. 'Challenge him. Tell him the game's up.'

'A hell of a long ride,' Gallant said. 'Sean Dolan said Flint's on his way to Washington.'

'Of course he did,' McCrae said excitedly, 'but we took it the wrong way. What Dolan meant is Flint's on his way to high office: he'll be the next senator for Kansas.'

'Oh, glory be! Now I've thought of something else,' Gallant said softly. He hurled away the stick he'd been using to poke the fire, sent it spinning into the shadows. 'Don't know where I heard it, but Flint's second wife was a fair-haired woman.'

McCrae looked puzzled.

'There's a fifty-fifty chance the son took after his mother,' Gallant explained. 'If Flint wanted me out of the way and concocted that elaborate frame-up, he'd need somebody to do the dirty work. Keeping it in the family would make good sense, and we've only Sean Dolan's word that the stepson was never at home. So what we need is Flint's second wife's maiden name.'

'That's easy, ' Melody said, 'because there'll be paper records. If they got married in church there'll be a register, there'll be a marriage certificate—'

'Forget the register,' Gallant said. 'For that we'd have to find the church, and why go to all that trouble when we know damn well where we'll find the woman's marriage lines.'

'So, first thing in the morning,' McCrae said, 'we head for Wichita—'

'We go nowhere; you two have already done more for me than I can ever repay.' Gallant, already up on his feet, shook his head. 'This is my fight. I tackle Flint, and I do it not in the morning, but now. . . .'

He was stopped by the sudden crackle of branches. But this time it was no predatory animal – it never had been, he realized – and it was close, too close. Boots crunched on crisp dead leaves, there was the metallic clack of a weapon being cocked.

Then a fierce shout seemed to set the shadows trembling.

'You'll tackle nobody,' Marshal Cole Banning yelled. He stepped out of the shadows and into the circle of firelight. 'The only place you're going, Gallant, is back to jail.'

He was still shouting harsh words, ordering Gallant to throw his gun to the ground and reach for the sky, when Deacon came out of the trees on the other side of the fire and Madison appeared over the crest directly above them, his angry gaze fixed on Melody Lake.

NINETEEN

If I'm held this time, Gallant thought, *that's the end of my stirring adventures in the American West.* He was as good as surrounded, and this time there was no cavalry to come charging over the hill. But, he realized, that knowledge would make Banning and his trusty side-kicks overconfident. They would be expecting capitulation, so, to shatter that confidence, he must hit them with the unexpected. While the cavalry wouldn't be coming over the hill, two foot soldiers were there by the fire and could be trusted to make nuisances of themselves.

Talking of fire, he recalled, with a feeling close to exultation, that Ted Bullock had stuck his oar in when Madison was being a nuisance in the smithy, and he'd done it by making use of the hot charcoal in the forge.

If that had worked for the blacksmith. . . .

Seconds had passed. Cole Banning was watching Gallant, but his attitude was relaxed; he fully expected the man he considered to be an effete Englishman to give up his weapon without a fuss. When Gallant lightly touched his hand to the butt of his six-gun and took a step forward the marshal followed the movement with his eyes, but showed no concern.

But the move for the gun was a deliberate ploy to draw the marshal's gaze. Cole Banning was watching Gallant's hand, waiting for the weapon to be drawn and dropped. Instead, Gallant presented him with the unexpected. With only the shortest of back lifts, he swung his leg at the fire. There was a minor explosion of sound and, trailing smoke and flame, most of the campfire flew at Banning. He ducked, flung up an arm to protect his face, tripped and fell over backwards – and Gallant was away and gone.

He ran out of the woods and sprinted through the wet grass on the fringes of the stand of trees to where the horses were tethered. Behind him he heard a loud bellow of anger or pain. A grim smile creased his face as he tried to imagine what tricks Melody and Stick McCrae were up to. Then he reached his horse. It had watched him coming. The whites of its eyes could be seen in the gloom. It was only lightly tethered. A flick of Gallant's hand released the reins from the low branch. He swung himself into the saddle, wheeled his horse towards the east and was touching the willing beast lightly with his spurs when the first shot cracked.

But it was the first and last shot fired by a town marshal who knew he was wasting effort and good shells. Gallant was already out of six-gun range, and exultant. To compound Banning's problems, he and his deputies had left their horses a long way down the hill on the Dodge City side of the woods. Their intention had been to proceed on foot, clawing their way up through trees and undergrowth, reaching Gallant by stealth and catching him unprepared.

Melody Lake had been seen leaving town. Banning had quickly located his two deputies, and the three men had followed the young woman. A fat lot of good it had done them. Gallant was racing through the night on a horse that was fresh and full of running. There was now nothing to stop him reaching the Guthrie spread, confronting the politician and, if he was correct in his suspicions, blowing away the dark shadow of the noose that had hung over him for too long.

Born Gallant had fully expected McCrae and Lake to make what he would have called confounded nuisances of themselves to help him in his dash for freedom. He would not have been disappointed.

Of the three lawmen Banning made the quickest recovery, and he was away after Gallant with the smouldering embers of the campfire still clinging like hot leeches to his vest and pants.

He was a big man, unstoppable, so Stick McCrae let him go. He had eyes only for Deacon. The deputy's instinct was to follow his boss. But apparently he had more intelligence than his appearance suggested: he knew instinctively that going after Gallant was a waste of time, and the sudden thud of hoofbeats and the single shot that followed settled it.

Madison was picking his way carefully down the slippery, leaf-covered slope from the crest, heading towards Melody Lake. His intentions were unclear, but there was an angry red weal across his exposed throat that suggested he could still feel the effects of her murderous stranglehold and was bearing a massive grudge.

Melody was a shrewd young woman, able to weigh up a situation at a glance. She didn't allow the angry deputy to get anywhere near her. She drew back her arm and flung her still half-full coffee cup in the same way as she had thrown the rock. Madison saw it coming in plenty of time, and ducked. The cup missed his head, carried on and clanked against a rock. Warm coffee splashed his face, his eyes.

Pressing her advantage, Melody stepped past McCrae and snatched the coffee pot from the bent branch that held it over the fire. Before the hot handle could sear her skin, she sent the pot spinning towards Madison.

This time his reactions were too slow. With his hand still scrubbing at his eyes, he tried desperately to avoid the spinning black pot and its scalding contents – and stumbled into its path. When the pot hit his shoulder, most of the near-boiling contents drenched his bruised neck. He let out a roar of anger and pain, then snapped his teeth shut and sat down hard.

They were posed like that, three contestants in a violent game that had reached an impasse, when Cole Banning returned. He stopped six feet from the fire and stood with hands on hips; then he gestured for his two deputies to back off. Unlike Madison's, his anger was cold, controlled.

'Where's Gallant going?'

McCrae waved a hand vaguely. 'Anywhere that's a long way from here.'

'I think you know. You two are as thick as thieves. And what the hell were you playing at? You helped a wanted man escape, in the process damn near killing two lawmen.'

Goodness, Melody Lake thought, *he knows.* Amusement tickled her. Her gaze wandered to Madison. He was glowering. She let her smile surface, and gave him a cheeky wink.

'Do you think I'm stupid, Lake?' Banning's sharp eyes had caught the interplay. 'On his way to Kansas City in a buckboard, Gallant got away from his escort. With help. That escort, two of my men, went missing. You, Lake, walk into my office with some fairy story of falling off your horse. Then my deputies show up, bruised and battered. And now, for Christ's sake, you're *all* here, all showing injuries of some kind – and you think I can't make a simple two plus two add up to four?'

'What do you intend doing with us?' McCrae said.

'Nothing. That comes later. The questions I ask then and how you and Lake answer could put both of you in jail. But it's Gallant I want, he's a killer, he'll hang – so for the last time, where is he going?'

'He's going to talk to the man who planned the killing of Senator Morton Slade,' Melody Lake said. Banning swung on her, frowning.

'What? You're saying Gallant was paid to kill the senator?'

140

'It wasn't Gallant. Some time ago a man commissioned your town blacksmith to forge a knife-blade for him and to fit a fine bone-and-leather handle. He had nothing planned, simply wanted a good knife. But he resembled Born Gallant in a way that would at once be noticed by a stagecoach driver fond of strong drink. That resemblance would be almost perfect if the man then adopted a certain manner of speech.'

She paused, watching Banning think his way to what she meant. 'And so,' she said carefully, 'in the mind of an important Kansas man who was looking to his future and saw the possibilities, a plan took shape.'

'So who is this feller with the knife?'

'He and the man who concocted the killing plot are very close.'

'That's the evasive answer of a politician.'

'At heart I'm a lawyer.'

'And not answering the question, when I want names.'

'Oh, but I've got a much better idea.'

'Names, not ideas.' Banning's gaze was dismissive. 'You've come up with a campfire yarn. You're telling lies to help Gallant, wasting my time, trying my patience.'

'We'll take you to him. To this man who hired another with a very special knife and appearance to remove a third man who was standing in his way.'

Madison snorted. He'd regained his feet. The coffee had soaked his shirt. One side of his neck was scarlet. His lips were tight with pain.

'She'll talk all night, Banning, getting ever more

complicated, stopping you in your tracks. Gallant's on a fast horse. By the time she's done he'll be in Texas and heading south.'

Banning had begun pacing, his boots scattering leaves, twigs, embers smouldering in the grass. He whipped off his hat, dragged a hand down over his face. He stopped, glared.

'That's not going to happen, because I'm not listening to any more made-up stories—'

'Oh, but you should,' Lake said. 'If Gallant gets a trial it'll be in a kangaroo court held in a saloon. Convicted before he's tried, hanged at dawn next day. If he's put before one of those courts I'll make damn sure I'm there to defend him, Banning.' She smiled sweetly. 'I'll tear your evidence to shreds. Gallant will walk free, and you'll be the laughing-stock of Dodge City.'

'Because I'll make damn sure the fiasco gets a big front-page spread in the *Dodge City Times*,' McCrae added. 'You'll lose your job, you'll be a swamper cleaning out saloons – and all that because you're too stubborn to listen to reason.'

'Pretty pictures, but if you're both in jail, none of them will get painted,' Banning said through clenched teeth. 'All right.' He held up a hand, silencing any retort. 'All right, if you know where Gallant's going and you can take me there, then I'm with you. Have to be. I don't trust you – but I've got no choice.'

'I hope to God all this talking hasn't delayed us for too long,' Melody Lake said softly. 'I know Gallant's character. It's not in him ever to consider that his actions can put him in danger. But he's heading into the unknown, into trouble, to clear his name. He expects Flint—'

'Flint?' Banning said, eyes widening in shocked disbelief.

'That's right, Guthrie Flint. The secret's out. We know from experience that he's a very dangerous man. If we're right, he's also the man behind a gruesome murder. Gallant is expecting him to be on his own, because that's the way that ambitious politician lives. But he won't be alone. So for your sake, Banning – as the town marshal trying to put an innocent man on the gallows – let's keep our fingers crossed that we get there before the bullets start flying.'

TWENTY

As had happened on other occasions, before his knowing the name of the man who owned the place, Gallant's ride towards Wichita took him past the Dolan spread. There was no moon. The house on the hill high above the ranch yard was a dark shape with hard outlines made visible by a ragged backdrop of trees of a lighter shade. No lights shone in the windows, though a glint of reflected light showed their position. The big house looked unoccupied, just as it had when he and Stick McCrae had tied their horses and gone in over the fence. That time, Dolan had been in his kitchen, so the lack of lamplight meant nothing.

And now? Well, now Dolan was of no interest. Gallant was pushing his horse hard along the opposite tree-covered ridge that overlooked the ranch yard. His thoughts were some way ahead, with a man called Guthrie Flint.

He realized he was on shaky ground. Together he, Stick McCrae and Melody Lake had come up with some facts and a lot of what could be wild guesswork. Guesswork wasn't enough to convict an important man of a terrible crime, as the lawyer in Melody Lake would understand all too well. Guthrie Flint had money, he had influence, and he was almost certain to have the backing of prominent members of local and national government.

Trouble was, even if, somehow, Gallant established that Flint's second wife's maiden name was Weston, that proved nothing. The knife used to murder Senator Slade had been picked up by stagecoach driver Stan Coleman, and was now wrapped in a bandanna in Gallant's saddlebag. But there was nothing to prove that the Frank Weston who got blacksmith Ted Bullock to make that knife was Flint's stepson. Even if he was, and had inherited his mother's fair hair, there was still no proof that Guthrie Flint was in it up to his neck, or even knew that his stepson was planning a killing.

As he pushed his horse on through the night Gallant was forced to admit that he could be on the wildest of all wild-goose chases. Then he chuckled softly into the chill breeze. Devil take the hindmost, nothing ventured nothing gained – weren't those the age-old sayings he had used often to boost his spirits, to push him on when doing so seemed futile? To hell with marriage lines and maiden names. He'd brazen it out. Knock on Flint's front door, walk in and show him the knife. Say, 'I believe this belongs to your stepson.'

But there was another, much more dramatic way to proceed, of course, for hadn't he said to Stick and

Melody when he was given the knife that, at some time in the near future, he'd find a use for it? And use, in Gallant's opinion, was much more effective than show.

Especially when that use created high drama.

Well, that time had come. Exactly how he would use that killing Bowie knife had just then dawned on Gallant, like the first rays of light seen on the horizon after a long, dark night.

He approached the Guthrie residence in the same way as he had when he and Stick McCrae had suffered ignominy and injury at the hands of Chet Eagan and his two cronies. Through woods thick with under-growth – Lord, was he for ever doomed to ride where riding was nigh-on impossible? – out into the open and down the grassy slope to the dirt drive and then the open space of the yard. Unlike Sean Dolan, Guthrie didn't earn his living from cattle, so 'ranch' was merely a name from the past for a current politi-cian's bolt-hole; a place of retreat from his Wichita offices which, if Gallant was unsuccessful, would soon be abandoned in his move to a plush office suite in Kansas City.

A senator's perks, bestowed on a truly sinful man if Gallant and his merry friends had got it right.

This was no house on the hill. The location chosen by the man who built the ranch was a shallow basin at the end of a valley, the house stood across the yard from the big barn, which Gallant had last entered unconscious and belly-down across his own horse. The warm yellow glow of oil lamps could be seen through the downstairs windows. A shadow moved across one of those windows. It could have been anybody or nobody: a change of light caused by a draught moving a lamp's flame. There were no horses at the hitch rail, which told Gallant nothing. He vaguely recalled stables somewhere on the spread, and there was always the barn to keep animals comfortable and out of sight.

The moon was still hidden behind heavy cloud cover. The empty hitch rail was there for Gallant's use. He rode in silently out of convenient darkness with just the tinkle of bridle metal and the pad of his horse's hoofs on muffling dust. Dismounted. Tied his horse. Checked his six-gun. He unbuckled his saddle-bag and took out the bandanna-wrapped killing weapon. The faintest of reflections on the broad, shiny blade matched the icy gleam in Born Gallant's blue eyes. He discarded the bandanna. Flipped Frank Weston's knife into the air and caught it expertly by its hefty blade. Walking with no more than a whisper of sound from his clothing and the faint creak of old dry timber held by rusty nails, he went up the steps and across the gallery to the front door.

He used the knife's hilt to announce his presence, pounding the heavy wood with force intended to startle; to shock; creating thunder to rock the guilty off their perch of complacency.

The response was instant.

'What the hell! Who is that?'

Guthrie Flint. His deep and angry voice coarsened by cigar smoke and strong drink, asking a question that went unanswered. The voice carried, as a politician's must, but he was as silent as Gallant in his movements: there was no more sound from the house until a bolt was hurriedly drawn and the door was snatched open.

The big man's face was flushed. His feet were bare. His shirt was bulging white over his paunch. His trousers, held up by a leather belt in the region of his hips, were partly covered by a purple Paisley dressing robe with the sheen of silk. No weapon, Gallant noticed. Well, why would there be? But no sign of alarm, either, no hint of panic.

Why was that? For an instant all the unease was with Gallant as his supreme confidence seemed questionable.

He braced himself.

'Damn late, I know,' he said, playing the fool and flashing a grin, 'Frightfully sorry and all that, but I knew you'd want to return this hideous pig-sticker to its rightful owner.'

He brought the knife from behind his back, lifted it, waggled it in front of Flint's narrowing eyes. Then, moving fast, he stepped over the threshold. He stiff-armed the politician out of the way. The big man cursed. Off balance, he stumbled back, banging his head hard against the wall. Gallant drew back his right arm. Like a knife-thrower performing in a touring circus, he flicked his wrist and sent the knife spinning end over end across the big room.

The layout of Guthrie's familiar living room had been clear in Gallant's mind. He'd known that across the room from the front door, on the far side of plump easy chairs and oak tables, there was another door leading to the house's interior. The knife flew towards those dark oak panels. It was a heavy weapon. There was a discernible whisper of sound as it disturbed the warm air. The whirling blade winked brightly in the glow of the oil lamps. Its flight from hand to target was unerring.

It took little more than a second for the knife to split the air on its way across the room. But it had scarcely left Gallant's hand before the oak door ceased to be the target. The door was flung open. A man with a six-gun in his hand was exposed. Blue eyes under lank fair hair caught the flicker of movement in the lamplight. There was no time to react. With the peculiar sickening thud of metal cutting into skin, flesh and bone, the knife hit him. Gallant had thrown with skill. The point of the knife pierced clothing and skin. The blade buried itself in the man's chest. He went over backwards. The six-gun flew from his hand, shattered a crystal decanter and fell to the floor in a shower of glass and expensive whiskey.

There was a moment of stunned silence, of utter stillness. The air stank of spilled whiskey. Guthrie Flint's florid countenance had turned pale. Gallant was finding it difficult to recover from the immense shock of unintentionally killing a man by an insane act of bravado. When he had recovered and was able to look the politician in the eyes, he detected in them a gleam of something like triumph.

That suspicion was confirmed when Flint spoke.

'Oh dear,' he said, speaking softly as he moved away from the open front door, away from Gallant. 'Now you really have cooked your goose, my boy. You've murdered the one man who could have saved your skin.'

'Is that an admission of your guilt? Your stepson killed Slade to remove the one obstacle barring you from high office?'

'Good Lord, no; no politician ever admits any-thing.' He smiled. 'But Marshal Cole Banning in Dodge City will learn from me that you forced your way into my house, assaulted me,' he ostentatiously massaged the back of his head, 'then murdered my stepson with the same weapon you used to kill Slade.'

'Your stepson's knife. What was I doing with it?'

'You stole it from this house when I offered you and your friends my hospitality. I freely spread the word, six months ago, that you passed this way in the days when you were looking for the killer of Slade's son. I will admit to the marshal that I've lived to regret my generosity: unknown to me you were a cheap thief, and a cold-blooded killer.'

'Wrong on both counts, of course, but what does it matter when I'm free to walk out of here and continue the fight?'

'If there ever was a fight in which you stood any chance,' Guthrie Flint said, 'it's here now, in this house, and it's over.'

'Flint, you're big, you're fat, you're out of shape and you're unarmed—'

150

Gallant broke off, the words dying in his throat. A violent blow between the shoulder blades drove him forward into the room. The effect was paralysing. The pain was instant and numbing. Suddenly he was unable to draw breath. He stumbled, went down on one knee. His attacker was behind him. Gallant was winded, strength leaking from muscles starved of oxygen. As vision blurred and consciousness began to fade, his subconscious took over. With his mouth open as he gasped for air, instinct made him drop his hand to his six-gun. He slapped empty leather.

When he twisted his head, strained to look up, dull-red fire pulsed behind his eyes. Through it he saw a tall man wearing a black Stetson so old it was turning green, clothing that was black and faded. He had a six-gun in its tied-down holster, its walnut butt polished to a high shine by use. In his hand he held the six-gun that he had plucked from Gallant's holster while delivering what was close to a knockout body blow. Guthrie Flint's pistol, taken by Gallant but soon to be returned to its owner, unless, . . .

'Chet Eagan,' Gallant croaked.

'Part repayment for that trouble in the barn, the kick in the face,' the gunman replied. 'I get paid in full when you hang by the neck.'

'That payday'll be a long time coming,' Gallant managed, biting back a groan of pain.

There was a fierce, nagging ache spreading outwards from between his shoulder blades. A .45 bullet in the back could have felt no worse. But he had been there many times: down in the sand of a foreign

151

desert; stoically contemplating death delivered by long muzzle-loading jezails; of being sliced to ribbons by robed assailants with curved scimitars.

Despite his torment, Gallant felt laughter bubbling. Compared to his previous travails this Kansas fracas was as nothing, kids fighting in the school playground. Drawing breath was painful, yes – but possible. Each drawn breath brought with it a return of strength. He had told Theodore Bullock he was a fast healer, and the same applied to his powers of recovery. Teeth clenched against pain, he struggled, pushed upwards and found his feet. He staggered but, recovered his balance with a hasty sideways step. He rested there, bent forward, head bowed, arms rigid and both hands clamped on his knees. He presented a picture of despair, a man physically battered and mentally defeated.

It was deliberate.

Play-acting. The posture adopted to create that pathetic image also put him in a position from which he could attack with power. As a young man he had played rugby at an English university. He had been a fierce tackler who had once broken an opponent's leg with his shoulder.

'Eagan, be careful,' Flint called.

But Eagan was grinning, overconfident, and Flint's warning came too late.

From the half-crouched position, Gallant flung his arms forward, then used the power of his leg muscles to launch himself almost horizontally at Chet Eagan. The man was fast, lightning fast. He managed a snap shot, but the trigger was jerked in panic. The bullet whined high and wide. Gallant thought he heard a cry from the living room. Then he ran at Eagan with the power of a charging bull, wrapped both arms around his thighs and lifted him off his feet.

Gallant ran him out of the house on to the gallery. A board splintered under his feet. He began to fall, dragged down by Eagan's weight. Then they both hit the boards. Eagan's body was ripped free of Gallant's iron embrace. The lean man rolled away, but his grip on Gallant's six-gun had been loosened. The weapon fell with a clatter, sliding towards the rail. Both men scrambled after it. Eagan, forgetting he had his own holstered pistol, got there first. Then Gallant was on him, landing on top of Eagan's bent figure as he scrabbled for a hold on the six-gun. Eagan touched it. His fingertips nudged the butt. The gun slid over the edge of the gallery and was gone.

'Clumsy,' Gallant chided. Then he grabbed a handful of hair, jerked Eagan's head back. There was a tearing sound as the scalp tore. Gallant was left holding a handful of hair. The pain drew a scream from Eagan. He abandoned all thought of weapons and rolled away. His eyes were screwed up, streaming tears. Both his hands clutched his bloody scalp.

Gallant sat down. He let his back rest against the gallery rail, gasping as pain knifed from his back all the way through to his chest. He looked down at the glittering metal of Guthrie's pistol, lying in the dust of the yard, a long way beyond his reach.

'Could have used it to kill him,' a voice called,

'which wouldn't have changed anything because a man can't be hanged twice.'

'Never mind Eagan, what happened here will make both of us happy men,' Gallant said, squinting sideways as Marshal Cole Banning came running up the steps. 'You won't make a serious mistake, and I won't hang – not even once.'

He reached a hand up to the rail, dragged himself to his feet. None of those involved in the desperate battle for survival being fought on the Flint property had heard the horses being ridden fast down the hill, into the yard. There were five of them. Gallant felt a surge of relief as Stick McCrae and Melody Lake followed Banning on to the gallery. Behind them, Deputies Deacon and Madison stayed were they were: mounted and well back across the night darkness of the yard. Watching and waiting, Gallant surmised, on the slim chance that he would again make a run for it.

'Where's Guthrie Flint?'

'Inside with a dead man,' Gallant said wearily.

Eagan had climbed to his feet and was leaning against the gallery rail, looking sick. Banning had walked over to him, and without evoking any protest had taken the man's six-gun and tossed it over the rail towards his two deputies.

Gallant watched without caring, concerned with his own pain and what the future held. He set off into the house ahead of Banning, ignoring the lawman's drawn Colt. Flint was slumped in one of the plump armchairs. He was clutching his arm, the shirtsleeve was soaked in blood. His face bore the shine of sweat.

His gaze expressed immense relief when he saw Banning and the badge gleaming on his vest.

'Thank God!' he said. 'This man, this . . . this sonofabitch . . . he broke in, murdered my stepson with that goddam knife, then tried his best to kill me. . . .' Then he stopped.

Frank Weston had appeared, stumbling in the interior doorway, and leaning against the jamb. From his neck to the belt at his waist the front of his shirt was blood-soaked; his face was that of a man close to death. In his shaking hand he clutched the big knife by its wet, slippery hilt. Somehow, agonizingly, he must have drawn it from his body, in his distress not realizing that the heavy blade had been plugging the wound, restricting the life-threatening flow of blood.

There sounded the sudden thud of feet as McCrae and Lake rushed to his aid. McCrae grabbed him as his legs gave way and he began to fall. He eased him down on a fancy chaise-longue. Blood began soaking into the dusky-pink brocade. Melody Lake knelt by the bloody figure. She glanced back, reached up and ripped the bandanna from the startled McCrae's neck. She folded it into a thick, soft pad and pressed it against the gaping wound that could be seen through the rent in Weston's shirt.

'Am I. . . ?'

Melody looked at McCrae. It seemed to Gallant that a silent message passed between the two. Then McCrae nodded.

'Yes,' Melody said quietly to Weston. 'I'm a lawyer but I've had medical training. I'm not going to lie to you. I'm sorry. I really can't see you pulling through.'

'So . . .' Weston said. His grin was sickly, his voice a whisper. 'Then it's time the truth came out.'

'Don't be a damn fool, Weston—'

'Shut up,' Banning snapped, and Guthrie Flint sagged back in the chair. 'Gallant,' Banning went on, 'get over there against the wall, lock your hands behind your head.'

He'd been in worse positions, Gallant thought, complying, and Weston was clinging on to life, there was hope yet – but what would be his story?

'I killed Senator Morton Slade,' Frank Weston said.

Banning shook his head stubbornly. 'Born Gallant killed Slade. He used the same knife on you.'

'Threw it. I opened the door at the wrong time—'

'There's a witness saw him knifing Slade.'

'No.' Weston shook his head weakly. 'Flint, my step-father, was after Slade's position. He wanted that man to take the blame,' he waved weakly at Gallant, 'because he knew that as a friend of Slade's he'd go after the killer.'

'The man's raving, off his head,' Flint snapped.

Banning held up a hand, again warning the politician. He looked with scepticism at the dying man.

'And then what? You were made to look like Gallant, talk like him. . . ?'

'He's lying,' Flint said. 'He's always hated me, sponged on me when I'd allow it; this is his way of getting back—'

'I told you, shut up,' Banning said.

'Deathbed confession,' Weston rasped, weakening.

'Which makes what he said the truth,' Melody Lake said to Banning, 'even if what I said was a lie.' She smiled at Weston, gripped a hand slick with blood. 'You're weak as a kitten, feller, but if we get you to a doc you'll live to be an old man.'

'But. . . ?'

'The knife hit soft tissue, missed vital organs.' She flashed another look at Banning. 'He didn't know that. He listened to me and thought he was a goner.'

'Of course he did, but dying or not it's his word against Flint's,' Banning said. 'This . . . this Weston, I don't know him. Guthrie Flint is a respected—'

'If you want proof,' Weston whispered, 'go talk to the stagecoach driver. Go talk to Stan Coleman.'

'We've done that,' Banning said flatly. 'Coleman was the witness; he saw the marshals gunned down, Slade knifed by Gallant.'

'He told lies for hard cash. Just like me,' Frank Weston said. 'Stan Coleman was paid by Flint.'

From the depths of the plump armchair Guthrie Flint leaned forward and put his face in his hands. Blood from his sleeve dripped steadily on to the floor. He uttered a long, drawn-out groan of anger and despair as the position in government that he had coveted drifted for ever out of his reach.

EPILOGUE

Born Gallant walked out of the Dodge City cell at ten the next morning. He passed Stan Coleman in Banning's office. The little stagecoach driver was clumping in, escorted by Madison and Deacon and smelling sourly of whiskey. What did a man get in the West, Gallant wondered, for telling lies for cash? Knuckles rapped? It all depended, he supposed, on the outcome: the man Coleman had been paid to frame for murder was walking free.

Banged into a cell in the pre-dawn chill, Gallant had been visited by Melody Lake and Stick McCrae. Little had been said, and what came out of that little was mostly sadness. Melody admitted somewhat sheepishly that she was returning to Kansas City. She would live with her parents, and resume her career as a lawyer. McCrae was staying put in Dodge City until the *Times*'s editor, Tom Caton, could find a replacement reporter. The cuts and bruises they had suffered in the most recent encounters were healing, scars fading, but both of them appeared to have had their fill of blood-soaked adventures littered with the bodies of dead men. They found it difficult to meet Gallant's eyes.

As for Gallant? He slept until the sun had warmed the streets, woke when Banning unlocked his cell, and walked out as a free man who had reached no decision. He crossed the boardwalk and angled across the street to Jake's livery barn to collect his gelding, thinking idly that he needed fresh challenges to replace those that, in Melody's words, he'd come through by the skin of his teeth. Every damn one of 'em.

Jake, the old hostler, having saddled his gelding and handed it over in exchange for silver coins, looked contemplatively at Gallant. What he said next gave Gallant the germ of an idea.

'Ain't you that feller got flogged?' Jake queried, scratching the thin white hairs clinging to his brown scalp. 'Me, I thought that was a punishment handed out to sailors on them pirate ships down there off the Spanish Main. Cat o' nine tails – ain't that what's used?'

'I am, and it is,' Gallant said, 'and I'm extremely grateful to you for mentioning it, Jake. Been wondering what to do, where to go, don't you know. I rather like this nag. Tell me, d'you think it'll make it to California?'

'Fed, watered and treated right,' the hostler said, 'a good horse with heart'll go anywhere, do 'most anything asked of it.'

'Rather like myself,' Gallant said, gathering the reins. He thanked the old man and was grinning like a fool as he rode out into the sunlight. When he turned his mount towards the Dodge City limits his blond head was uplifted, his blue eyes gazing into the far distance. He might have been heard murmuring to himself:

'Madcap idea, Gallant old chap, but I'll miss Melody and Stick damnably and I always did fancy sailing round the Horn. Before the mast, and all that rot. Head for San Francisco harbour, sign on as a deck hand, work my passage south to where the southern ocean runs wild and untamed.

'Think it's called a sabbatical,' he continued to murmur as he left the town behind him. 'Wonder if that means I'll be back?'